COLIN BEAZLEY

WITHIN THE MIST

FOUR BOYS BOOKS

First published in Great Britain in 2013

Copyright © Colin Beazley 2012

The moral right of Colin Beazley to be identified as the author of this work has been asserted in accordance with the Copyright, Design and Patents Act, 1988

All rights reserved. No part of this publication may be reproduced or transmitted in any form or by any means, electronic or mechanical, including photocopy, recording, or any information storage and retrieval system, without permission in writing from the publisher.

British Library Cataloguing-in-Publication Data
A CIP record for this title is available from the British Library

ISBN 978-0-9571396-2-6

Published by
Four Boys Books
Heywood House
Chulmleigh
Devon
EX18 7QS

Resemblance in some instances to actual people living or dead, or locales is purely coincidental.

'hark, now hear the sailors' cry,
smell the sea, and feel the sky,
let your soul and spirit fly,
into the mystic . . .'

- Van Morrison

Illustrations by the author

ALSO BY COLIN BEAZLEY

One Day in June

A Tale of Two Elephants

Silly and Not So Silly Verse

DOON

1944

Within The Mist

Chapter 1

Nothing stirs. The patchwork roofs of riven Welsh slates are black with the early morning dew. A solitary gull caws, perched on one needle-thin, pink leg, high on top of a terracotta chimney pot. Windows, dark and cold, showing nothing, seeing nothing, wait to greet the day. No doors creak, no one alights from their bed, no soul stirs; not even a dog stretches or yawns in its basket. All is still, dead to the world in this small, sleepy, fishing village of higgledy-piggledy cottages that is Doon.

The day had awoken and risen before anyone. The emerging sun dramatically skirted the distant, glassy horizon, its silent, rejuvenating rays heralding the start of another day. Yet on the broad, shingle foreshore, looking out across the English Channel, a chilled sea breeze and mist moved lightly amid the tussocks of marram grass growing in the high dunes.

Dilly would come to this beach early every morning before preparing her father's breakfast and just daydream, imagining herself miles away across the shimmering sea in a world far removed from her mundane life. Today though, the elements had conspired to keep from her that enduring sense of optimism she usually felt. A thick, milky-white sea mist rolled and swirled towards the desolate beach: the mist's ghostly and overwhelming presence always unsettled her. All seemed lost; the advancing and retreating waves appeared now still – the sparkling surf gone. No sound, no sight, just a deafening silence and an obscure damp veil, all consuming, all invading, swallowing everything as it tumbled ashore. Even the call of the sea birds had deserted this place. The cold air bit into her face. Dilly hated days such as this: it unnerved her and made her feel as if the world was closing in on her and, for a brief instant, she was uncertain if she was alone on her beach.

The deep shingle scribed a lazy curve, stretching from beyond the mysterious and secret Listening Station west for some three or four miles, reaching out into the sea to Worlds End. Formed by the only rocky outcrop on this part of the coast, Worlds End promontory was dominated by the old light standing one hundred and fifty feet tall: a witness to eighteenth-century engineering and to the dangerous waters which lay offshore. However, today its lamp would prove of no value. Only the deep drone of its foghorn would alert passing craft to what otherwise might spell their premature end.

At the light's foot, a squat, white-washed cottage was perched above the threatening sea, and way off along the rocks, the enormous foghorn trumpet of the lighthouse sat, its black mouth gaping towards the distant horizon. Dilly had spent her entire life in this cottage: twenty-two years of wonderful memories, as well as sorrow and heartache. In her early years, disaster had struck, stealing away her beautiful mother, a tragedy Dilly found hard to bear. Father retreated into himself, spending more time tending to the lamp and busying himself with keeper's duties.

The vast, coastal wasteland held the only escape for her each day. Here she felt safe, rediscovering its rich and abundant wildlife which, as a child with her mother, she had learnt to treasure. Here they had so often strolled over the marshes and dunes. For Dilly the fierce and unforgiving winters proved exhilarating: their winds purged the land, destroying and rebuilding the dune-scape. The surging tides and their ensuing longshore drift shifted the shingle ridges continuously, re-shaping the beach. During that season few others ventured there. It was her world and that excited her; no one else could ever begin to understand exactly how important this place was.

The foghorn boomed, resounding through the mist, its long, solemn drone seeming to squeeze the very air about her. The sudden blast, although expected, had still come as a surprise to her and for one brief moment in the silence that followed, Dilly believed she heard the sound of something or someone moving on the beach, way out towards the point. Concentrating hard she heard nothing. The mist must be playing tricks on her; it was uncanny how it would do that. But, sure enough, there was the noise again: distant but getting nearer. Now she was certain. Someone was coming along the beach towards her. The steps were slow and methodical. Walking on the loose and ever moving stones was not easy and quite exhausting, the smooth, oval pebbles making progress laborious. Her heart quickened as a figure appeared out of the lingering mist: a wiry young man whom she had never seen before. Snuggling lower amongst the sparse vegetation at the crest of the beach, a feeling of vulnerability overcame her; she felt threatened and hoped her presence would not be discovered. From her refuge she observed the fair-haired man striding out purposefully between the strandline of plants and the wash in the direction of the fisher-huts and the Listening Station beyond, oblivious to anything and everything. Then, as quickly as the swirling mist had let him through, so it mysteriously swallowed him back.

The boom of the foghorn echoed yet again around the bay.

Chapter 2

As Dilly lay dreaming on the fine, white sand, excited by what her beach had revealed to her this day, Stella Smart stood at the end of the short jetty which reached out in the cove below Doon. She strained every sense to catch just a hint of her Archie's boat which was way out there somewhere, in the abyss. Often before sun-up he would head out, motoring around the point into the big bay, and set his lines in the waters off the Listening Station some mile or so out. The Boil was the area where the sewage and warm outwash from the Listening Station stirred the depths and created an ideal feeding ground for the fish. Here in this great sea store of food they would gorge themselves on the sprats that fed on the plankton bloom there. She had not expected to see his boat in this weather and, listening as hard as she might, there was no sound of its engine. He'd not set sail home until he'd got a full catch, but he was usually back by now. Never mind, he could look after himself: his father and grandfather had made sure of that.

There was a time when four or five boats would set out from the cove each day to seek out new fishing grounds. It had been good for generations, but that was before the outbreak of war, and now Archie was the only fisherman left, the only one whose life and livelihood depended on the sea. The fishermen had become old men, sitting on the sea wall or jawing over a pint in the pub. The young lads had left the village, finding better paid jobs in the towns and city: jobs that weren't so hard and dangerous – that's if conscription had passed them by. Archie Smart was alone on his boat, apart from Billy Richards, an excitable thirteen year old who had no desire to make fishing his life, but just wanted to earn a bob or two.

"Archie'll be all right Stella, no worry," cried Jim over the sound of his clanking red post-bike and its squeaking brakes as he juddered to a halt outside the General Stores on the sea front. He rested its handlebars against the window, behind which Doris took particular pride in arranging her display of fare.

"I'd be obliged if you would remove your bicycle, Mr Postman," she would cry from inside. Although she knew his name full well, at moments such as these she preferred not to use the more familiar term of address. Irritated, but not surprised, he obliged and, whilst sorting out the village mail, shouted out again to Stella,

"He'll be back soon. He's bound to be with dirty weather like this." The sprung, brass doorbell tinkled above his head as Jim entered the store and made his first delivery of the day.

"Good morning Doris," he scoffed.

"It is indeed," she retorted smartly, "now you've got that contraption off my window."

Stella turned from her vigil and, pulling a knitted shawl up over her head, shivered, then scurried along the jetty and beside the sea wall to where her little cottage stood. It was one of three nestled between the store and the lane up to the church. There was a real urgency in her step as she stumbled over the cobbles, undoubtedly prompted by the possible imminent return of her husband. If she was quick she would be able to avoid any difficult confrontation and improbable explanation; life would be so much simpler and her secret would remain a secret!

Opening the stout, wooden gate to the cottage garden caused its hinges to squeak and she looked about anxiously before she entered. The low picket fence retained a rich jumble of marine bric-a-brac and antiquities in the front yard. A tired-looking crab pot with split, hazel bows sat on top of a bleached, wooden fish crate marked Crabester Fisheries. A large, spherical, ancient and crumbling steel buoy, riddled with rust, was in a pile with twenty or more cork floats, a length of hessian rope and a part deflated blue fender. A bent winch handle was propped up against a short wooden bench, the back of which was supported by the cottage wall. To complete the picture a leggy, fuchsia bush burst forth, crimson-red, from beside the front door.

The door had been newly coated in white by Archie when he had painted the picket fence, window frames and fascia boards of their stone cottage with the same paint. Stella rapped twice on the door pane which was rather strange as Archie, the cottage's only other occupant, was at sea. She lifted the latch and, deliberately opening it only part way, squeezed in, closing it firmly behind her. For a few moments afterwards hushed voices could have been heard from inside, had anyone been listening.

Outwardly the three fishermen's cottages looked much the same. Each boasted a pair of chimneys and one small skylight in the grey roof of large, thick, riven slates which looked as if they'd been bitten into shape.

Two meagre dormers upstairs sat above the lower windows which were either side of the front door. The other two cottages had low stone walls fronting them. History tells that Archie's dad, when returning from market one day, stopped at the pub to sup awhile. As he brought his cart back to the beach it ran away from him and demolished part of the wall of what then was his cottage. In a fit of temper he pulled down the remaining cobbles, casting them back on to the beach. Archie's ma was not having that so, when he'd sobered up, she forced him to make her a 'pretty' fence!

Each cottage had two pokey bedrooms upstairs with low, crippled ceilings and a snug and scullery downstairs. A tiny cooker which ran on bottled gas, a tin bath with a board on top that served as a kitchen worktop, a buff-coloured Belfast sink, a rickety cupboard and a table with benches furnished Stella's scullery. Their privy was out in a lean-to alongside the back door. The garden at the rear of the cottage was Archie's pride and joy. Lupins, dahlias and hollyhocks weren't his thing. The main loves in Archie's life were his fishing, especially his boat the *Lively Lady*, and his veg patch. Rows of regimented onions grew ever fatter, beans and peas struggled energetically skyward, plump spring cabbages and trenched-up tatties all awaited their fate on the plate.

The back door eased ajar, Stella peered out around it looking both ways and, only when she was assured no one was looking, opened the door right back stepping onto its threshold. Turning, she glanced indoors and, looking down, beckoned for something to come out. An overweight tabby strolled out, purring and sniffing the air. Stella, in a hushed voice, cursed the tiresome cat as she encouraged its saunter with her foot; it miaowed and scampered up the garden path, dragging its wallowing belly in the dirt.

A head poked out. There was no mistaking it: a man's head with curly, ginger hair, but, very strangely and rather peculiarly, it was only half-way up the door frame! Stella ushered her regular visitor out the door, as usual begging him to be as inconspicuous as possible although there was little point as most in the village, with the exception of Archie, knew what she was up to. Timothy was a 'little man', tiny in stature in fact, only four feet two inches tall. Stella resisted calling him Tim, conscious that when she found herself absorbed in wild and passionate love-making with him, she might prefix his name with 'Tiny' which would be unforgiveable and undoubtedly ruin the moment!

Timothy's age was hard to judge: his mature face appeared to contradict his exceedingly small stature so she thought maybe he was in his early forties. Actually he was thirty-six, but that would have made no difference to Stella who worked hard to disguise her fifty-five years. What was important to Stella was that he was good in bed: in fact, he was tremendous, but there again, to her mind absolutely anyone would be when compared to her Archie.

Nosey Marjorie Richards lent out from her upstairs window next door, and craned her long, scrawny neck so as not to miss the excitement of Timothy's escape.

"Away with you before he gets back," Stella implored, sweetly but firmly. Timothy pecked Stella on the cheek as she bent over, sniffed deeply her pungent perfume and then silently headed up the garden path. Just before he shinned over the wall into Maid's End Lane and up to the church, his secret assignation was broadcast to the world as he unwittingly trampled and crunched his way through Archie's pile of fresh, crab shells.

As a young slip of a lass, Stella had always been a fool for a handsome fellow and she wouldn't let anything or anyone get in her way of finding such a prize. It mattered not to her if they were courting or promised to another: forbidden passion was her carnal reward. She couldn't rightly recall how she'd ended up with Archie, but ended up with him she had. Stella discovered that everything that had ever thrilled and satisfied her in a man was not now evident in Archie – not that she was any spring chicken herself. Her once youthful figure and her good looks had given way to a fuller, bounteous figure: an appearance which was tired and ageing in a generous, floral-print, housewife's dress and pinny. In the past month her hair had started to come out in tufts on her hairbrush. She consoled herself by believing that she was more or less what many mature men yearned for, with the exception of her hair problem, and certainly it seemed to be just what lonely Timothy relished two days a week, regular as clockwork. Neither Timothy nor Stella cared exactly which one of them was short or which tall: when they were in bed making love, they were able to look right into each other's eyes.

Any magic which may have existed in her marriage had long since disappeared. Sharing a bed with Archie was like lying next to a beached whale of gigantic and blubbery proportions that wobbled with every breath, like some monster taking refuge beneath the same bed linen as her and stinking of fish! In spite of her depressing discovery, no protracted observations of the creature by eminent zoologists or marine biologists had materialized: quite the contrary. The beast lay contentedly undisturbed, showing no evidence that it would relinquish its place on 'her' mattress. Infuriating.

Every night when not sailing the wild seas, or basking in some exotic destination like the pub, this leviathan would be outstretched beside her, snoring, snorting and smelling.

The ever vigilant Marjorie Richards, glimpsing Timothy disappearing up the lane, straightened her head, retracted her giraffe-like neck and closed the window for another day.

Chapter 3

Within the hour Archie and Billy had retrieved their long lines, unhooked their catch from the hundreds of twisted gut snood lines, and lifted the 'dhan' marker buoys onboard. Archie brought *Lively Lady* about to a course westward, making for the safe harbour of Doon. Struggling to navigate his way home in this filthy, lingering fog, Archie knew full well that Stella and he were a lost cause. To leeward lay the long run of shingle and ahead the low, rocky spit and lighthouse that dominated it. The sea, which had until then offered only a light, ocean swell, strengthened as he headed out to windward, navigating to avoid the rocks of Worlds End. An all-pervading fog washed about the twenty-eight foot fisher, cloaking it in an eerie, yellow nothingness. Archie's experience and knowledge of these waters would once again ensure their safe passage.

Straining his eyes, he muttered, "'Tis bloody filthy, damn British weather."

Rounding the point, hugging close to the coast, the swell grew as the breeze picked up and Archie manoeuvred the little craft to avoid any risk of getting pushed onto the half-submerged rocky outcrops. As Billy tediously gutted and sorted the day's catch and coiled the lines in their baskets, gear and crates slid about the deck, not as violently as on some trips he had known but enough for him to realise the sea was becoming restless.

The aged craft was in first class order, Archie had seen to that, and after all, this was a trip he'd done hundreds of times before. There was nothing to worry about if he kept his head and relied on his ancient compass, speed log and unquestionable instinct. They'd spent several hours over the Boil during slack water, hopeful of a successful catch. The tide had long since turned, running now towards the beach.

A blast shook the air. It boomed over the roar of the sea and the throaty chug of *Lively Lady*'s smelly engine. Turning to where he thought the explosion had come from he saw nothing in the hanging fog. For one brief moment he thought, "After all we are at war," and pondered the chances of it being an enemy bomb, but why would the Germans bomb here? He wondered if it might even be a plane ditching.

Conscious that this was distracting him from the job in hand, he ignored these ludicrous ideas and the unexplained blast, and pushed on purposefully for Doon and its safe harbour. Archie knew full well in weather such as this that sounds can play funny tricks on you and was pleased he'd decided not to anchor up and sit out the rough weather. He had never enjoyed the luxury of being able to swim, so his cumbersome Mae West afforded the only hope if things went belly-up – if indeed he'd been wearing it. Even at this time of year the temperature of the waters hereabouts offered a meagre ten minutes or so before hypothermia started to take hold.

The stubby wiper on his aft wheelhouse's window pushed the moisture of the biting mist off the screen with every passing arc. He smeared the inside glass with the back of his hand, which squeaked as he did so, but the best visibility was when he ventured to stick his head out of the cabin. Another noise echoed overhead: this time it was the reassuring boom of the foghorn.

The lighthouse had been Seth's world for all his working life, nigh on forty years, and before him, that of his father. He knew little else, and on the occasions when the Most Glorious Trinity House, as it was referred to hereabouts, inflicted a relief keeper upon him, he would stay stubbornly at his station. Many boats over the years drifted past his high window on the world, but this day he would see none of them. The isolation of the light and the solitude of the job was something he loved and, consequently, the family had had to get used to. For his daughter Dilly, who had known no other way, it had been easy but not for her mother. She had been brought up in the nearby market town where life was very different, and had always been concerned that Dilly might miss out living in this remote place. Yet her endless pleading with Seth brought little change to their situation. When he could cope no longer with her nagging, as he regarded it, he'd head out of their cottage and climb the one hundred and sixty-nine cold, stone steps to take refuge in the Great Lens Gallery at the top of 'his giant lamp post on the rocks', as Dilly would like to describe it. There, day after day, he would scan the horizon through his brass telescope, hour after tireless hour. The weather played no part in this ritual: come rain, shine, storm and this impenetrable fog he would keep a waiting watch on the relentless, outstretched sea before him. He knew not when this vigil had started, but it was many, many years before, maybe back to when he first got his ticket and became a keeper. What he did know though, was why he did it.

In the fourteenth century the French sailed across the English Channel and invaded England, burning and pillaging the medieval market town from where his wife's family had hailed. If that wasn't enough, they were back in the July of 1545, thirty thousand of them in two hundred ships, just along the coast. The 'Frenchies' were gone by August but not until the British vice-admiral's flagship, the *Mary Rose*, had floundered and sunk. It may have been a long while ago but there was nothing to say that they wouldn't try again. If Seth had anything to do with it, enemies would not be landing on his beaches, invading the land and attacking the people he was now destined to protect at any cost. After all, someone had to keep a vigilant guard, ever ready to alert the authorities at the first signs of an invading armada. For Seth, always looking to the past, the years moved slowly, his life changing little: the threat was always there. War was a funny thing, he would muse, and if that wasn't enough, now of course there were the Germans. To him it was clear that you could never be too careful.

It was difficult to imagine what there would be to see of interest through a telescope in thick fog: certainly you could no longer see the giant, white cliffs that stood proud and high along the coast. For some the momentary reprieve from duty might prove a chance for self-contemplation, to pause from the great monotony of lighthouse life and to reflect on one's personal achievements and future opportunities. In Seth's case, however, more importantly it gave him a chance to have a snooze after a small tot of single malt. He adored the heavy, peat flavour and what was for some the unpleasant medicinal tinge, but above all he delighted in the way it helped him doze off. One thing was sure: he could not see Archie's fragile, clinker fishing boat surging for its port.

Spray washed over the boat's prow and windward gunwale, soaking Billy who hastily took refuge in the wheelhouse with Archie. As he entered, wiping the spray from his face, he cracked his head on the doorframe and words tumbled from his mouth, "Beggar me."

No one else heard his exclamation, but if they had they wouldn't have been surprised. It helped relieve Billy's anger if not his pain. Archie thrust into Billy's hand a mug of strong, steaming tea, freshly poured from a jug simmering on the small coal stove. They each devoured a wedge of cold potato pie, Stella's forte at this time of rationing, and much appreciated after hours out at sea in the cold and damp. *Lively Lady* motored at about five knots around the headland and on into the sheltered waters of Doonhaven. Archie turned her towards the beach, lining up her bow with the bright red phone box perched on the sea front, which he could faintly make out. Opening her up he powered for the steep, ridged foreshore, as if in an attempt to reach the very same phone box. He cut the engine a minute or two before the little craft's hull surged onto the polished, round pebbles which grated and cracked like toy marbles as the keel ploughed a fresh, deep furrow. The sheer weight and speed forced them sufficiently far, the bow coming to bear on a creaking, timber board embedded in the shingle. The timbers had not long since been greased so the *Lively Lady* slid freely some eight or so feet over two more groaning boards before finally coming to rest. Without a word a handful of old boys gathered as one of them steered an ancient tractor across the pebbles. A steel cable was hooked up and the exhausted Fordson, with great effort, proceeded to haul the *Lady* further up the beach and clear of the incoming tide.

The catch for Archie this day had been a fair one although several fish had been lost to market, half eaten by dogfish and being only good now for baiting Archie's pots. Having landed their catch, Archie and Billy shed their sou'westers, oil skins and leather thigh boots and headed off with the men of the village for The Ship. Here, oblivious to all, snug in his usual corner seat in the bar, sea water running in his veins, a pint of golden ale waiting to run down his throat, Archie drifted into a deep and well-earned sleep.

Chapter 4

Nazareth Josiah Greenwood, late of this parish, rested a mere three feet below his tombstone, and had done so for the past forty-one years. Above him, unconscious but not dead, lay Timothy, snoring contentedly, his back propped against the lichen-covered headstone which leant at a jaunty angle. This was not from the burden of Timothy's short body, but people in these parts were convinced that it had always been like that, saying the undertaker deliberately erected it thus to resemble the angle at which old Nazareth walked.

Timothy's slumbers were rudely curtailed, he knew not exactly by what. However, he did appreciate that a big, slobbering, affectionate black Labrador standing commandingly over him probably had something to do with it. Strands of glutinous saliva hung and dribbled from its jowls and, if that wasn't enough, seeing that the human was now well and truly awake, the beast started to lick his face with its monstrous, coarse, dripping tongue. Each lick delved deeper into Timothy's nose, ears and eye sockets with the mutt achieving almost complete coverage before it was finally pushed away in disgust.

By now the onshore fog had lifted and the day had developed into a bright if not breezy one, warm enough for Timothy to doze off again.

"Prince, home boy," came the cry, from way off in the corner of the churchyard. This once proud animal, limped towards its master apparently in pain. Close to where Prince's master waited, swirling fingers of wood smoke rose high above a smouldering bonfire. Like wisps of cotton wool they billowed, eddying upward then tumbling down on the breeze. Embers spiralled amid the smoke like confused fire flies lost in the smog, wondering where to go. The cracking of the twigs pierced the air as the fire took hold and the roar of the flames accompanied the spectacle as another gust lifted the blaze.

A tall, dark figure silhouetted against the sky stood attending to the fire with a long stick which on occasions he used to encourage the blaze. This was the Very Reverend Thomas Dunbar, vicar of this very troubled parish and spiritual leader of his wayward flock. He stood six feet one inch tall, erect and almost distinguished in appearance, still maintaining a hint of his boyhood good looks and charm. His once full build had now diminished, probably on account of worry and his erratic eating habits, reverting his form to being slight: a wisp of a man. Dunbar always dressed smartly, albeit in attire that sadly now looked shabby and long in need of a needle and thread. His face bore the haunting evidence of hard times, drawn and haggard, eyes deep set, his cheeks hollow and a forehead deeply furrowed. Weary, this godly man displayed no evidence of his holy eminence, except that is, for a pair of thin-rimmed gold halos which rested on the bridge of his wrinkled nose.

Here was a man who had a rare old chip on his shoulder: no one was too sure why. It may have been a result of his breeding, his youth spent growing up in Richmond, or perhaps his time at Eton, or joining his father in one of the successful city banks. It could, however, have been nothing more than his six years in the Royal Navy. Much more likely though was the forfeiting of a military career to join the ministry and eventually being side-lined to this out-of-the-way rural parish of Doon. Young curates in neighbouring churches came and went and nearly always, it appeared to him, ascended the clerical ladder.

Dunbar could be a bit prickly at times over his lack of prospects and certainly never discussed his past career. Needless to say, everyone had their own suspicions for his continued presence and would often be heard to openly air them down at The Ship. Knowing that proved irksome to Dunbar. In itself it didn't overly bother him, but being aware of so many personal and private details about each of them, whilst bound by the confidentiality of the cloth, tested his patience at times. Yet that did not prove to be the greatest test of Thomas's patience. The greatest test of his patience was his wife.

The confession he had shared with the compassionate Miss Philippa McWalters was all telling.

"In the early days of my ministry, whilst still a novice, an opportunity arose for me to attend an evangelical conference in eastern Africa. I knew little of African ways and far less of the church in this developing country. Uganda was a revelation to me: its abiding tribal culture, the wild enthusiasm for everything Christian and the heritage of hundreds of years of colonial rule. The preaching tour culminated in the capital, Kampala, at the Kolololo Full Gospel Community Church, and it was there that I met my wife-to-be. Precious found it difficult to settle back here. Being black made it hard to fit into conservative England and a rural way of life. She found it so different from what she was used to. We persevered and there were times when things seemed easier, but that was long before Precious became ill.

"To begin with, physically she appeared much the same, but slowly things changed, and for the worse. I never expected life to be so different. In the early days Precious would have occasional difficulty recalling things but it wasn't important or a particular problem and we got over it with a laugh or a joke. She started to forget our conversations and began repeating questions, and it was then that I realised something was really wrong. It was clear this was becoming apparent to her and proving irritating."

Here he paused, just for a few moments, probably to gather his thoughts and consider what he should say. More than likely, though, it was the memories of these times that disturbed him still.

"Over the following months she started to find it harder to do things, everyday tasks that had been part of our normal way of life. Even if she could do them, they would take a lot longer. She'd misplace things: keys, money, even food. We'd find vegetables hidden in the most unlikely places and even hot meals would go missing! All of this was hard, but the real problem for me came as her personality changed.

"Precious was never a moody woman, but she was proving increasingly so now, testing my patience to the limit. The local doctor, whom she no longer recognised, found it hard to be certain what exactly was troubling her and quite where all this would end, saying it was unusual for such a condition to strike someone so young. Both of us found it increasingly impossible to communicate effectively with each other, and our emotions ran high, as did our frustration. I knew her mother in Africa had suffered with a degenerative illness but never appreciated that Precious might be affected in the same way.

"Folks in the village couldn't help but notice something was very wrong. They avoided her, choosing to make conversation with only me should we meet and making their excuses to hurry away after services. No one was unkind, but no one helped, and all the time this terrible disease was taking a greater hold. The fits of violent anger, hallucinations and delirium bore heavily on me, as both physically and emotionally I found it increasingly harder to cope. Precious is lost to me; she has gone forever, and only her body remains with me lying in our bed. She will go days hardly eating anything, then gorge herself, even trying to eat the bed sheets and pillows. Should she rise, she will wander the room groaning and grunting and frightens me with her insane behaviour. She sees me no more, she doesn't know who I am. Her journey is soon coming to an end and her suffering will be over as she arrives in heaven – the dear Lord will see to that. But her going will have been a most painful one."

Dunbar, heavy of heart, engrossed in his lingering and painful bereavement, was unable to recollect those wonderful times of their early life together, those memories having faded with the passing of time, shot through by the stress and strife of it all. The only faint ray of hope on this earth of ours for Thomas was Miss Philippa McWalters, the village school mistress, bell ringer at the church and mature spinster of this said parish. If it wasn't for those brief and treasured moments after the Sunday mass, the Thursday night bell ringing practice and Dunbar's increasingly frequent contributions to the school's academic studies, dear Thomas's life would have proved almost intolerable. She was so full of vitality. Had Thomas married Pippa his life would have been oh, so very different.

The opalescence of the cloud-covered sky seemed to spread a canopy over the graveyard where Timothy lay, sleeping again. The bonfire was all but out, its flames having dwindled to a scarlet glow, its billowing smoke clouds now thin wisps drifting back and forth. Dunbar had long since gone, leading Prince away with the promise of a hearty feed and his basket for that post meal snooze in which all old dogs seemed to delight.

So it was for Thomas that just as his marriage to Precious had cast a long dark shadow over his life, his marriage to the church offered him solace, strength and meaning. The sense of its significance in his otherwise burdened existence grew almost daily. The church offered him a sanctuary, a holy place where he could find peace, something that was presently in short supply.

Dominant, grand and erect upon the gentle rise above the fishing settlement of Doon, proudly stood the edifice to the Lord of Saint Mary and Saint Michael. The church commanded a breath-taking view southwards, beyond the Light and across the Channel towards northern France, whilst all about unfolded the amazing beauty of the far-reaching countryside – fresh, verdant and with the promise of another rich bounty. The tower, a stout stone structure boasting a full three bells, proudly crowned this dramatic building. Its imposing southerly porch, with wooden medieval benches and a flagstone floor worn by the passage of feet over the years, welcomed parishioners and visitors alike, yet a sense of neglect hung over the building. Broken roof slates had slid from their rightful place, kept only from breakage by the gutters. Predatory ivy clung to the walls biting ever deeper into its historic structure. Inside the church the air was cold and hosted a faint, musty odour of damp. An elaborate and intricately carved medieval screen divided the chancel from the rest of the church, hiding the priest's door through which Dunbar would enter. A grey, lead font ringed with the signs of the zodiac, and a cold, white marble tomb were on full display, silhouetted beneath the magnificent Norman arches by the soft daylight which shone through the fine stained glass windows that adorned the church.

For many, this building was of little importance, representing a grand old monument beside which one could be buried in the fullness of time. For Thomas, however, it was much more than that: it was a mansion within which every moment could be cherished. Thomas's favourite place to meditate, when he got the chance, was in the chancel before the simple altar and below the lofty, high-arched stained glass window of the two saints. It was a window like no other in the church, coming alive with every passing cloud and ray of sun; the colours vibrant with each sunburst. It helped Thomas to feel alive again.

Oblivious to all, Timothy languished in his private world, dreaming. No one, not even Timothy, would know to what depths his dreams would descend, let alone if they would have a terrifying or happy end. One moment he'd be flying way up in the clear, blue sky, the next he'd be swimming way below in the deep, blue sea perhaps drowning, or was it just helplessly falling through the air, so fast he couldn't breathe. He really wasn't sure. Eventually he returned to earth, distraught, confused and still tired. Not all of Timothy's dreams were like this, or left him in such a state. In truth, most of his dreams revolved around women, or to be precise, searching for the love of a good woman who would care for him in a way that he had never known as a child. He was only too aware that for some his height, or lack of it, meant he didn't measure up, resulting in his bold advances being shunned. Fortunately, Stella didn't see it that way, and even when they were not lying together making love, she'd be thrilled when, standing before her, Timothy would bury his face between her bountiful breasts, so deep into her curvaceous cleavage that he could hardly breathe.

Timothy stirred: the evening was well on now, the day disappearing over the horizon beyond the deep sea. The damp night air chilled him. Picking his way between the headstones he clambered down, along Maid's End Lane, on towards the Listening Station. He cut off across the field track to where the fishermen's shacks stood above the long beach, and on to his ramshackle, wooden caravan sheltered behind the high dunes. Climbing the slatted steps he reached the low door, closing it behind him on the cold, inky darkness of another night.

Chapter 5

As the sun rose gloriously revealing itself above the long, lazy sea, the last remnants of the haze disappeared, giving way to the breezes which playfully chased wisps of white cloud high above the sparkling water.

The joy of a new day washed over Dilly as, barefooted, she paddled and splashed in and out of the foaming, white shallows, surf breaking all around her. Full of life, full of joy, she was a child again with a love for everything. Screeching gulls circled and swooped overhead, their spirited acrobatics making Dilly laugh with pleasure, and as she did, a thought came to her.

"This is my world. I love the wild seas and the flaming sunsets."

Feeling so blessed, she stopped, flung her arms high in the air and cried out, "This is my home."

The birds tumbled from their flight and then flew nervously off in every direction. Dilly looked skyward and called after them, "One day I too will fly away."

Along the shore, away from the village, past the weathered fishermen's shacks and the hut where the mysterious young man stayed, rested Timothy's dejected caravan, crouching low behind the dunes. Living in a world of the tall had not been easy for Timothy. What had started as the ideal childhood had developed into anything but. As a small infant he enjoyed being the focus of his dear mother's love and thrived on his father's playfulness and pride in him.

However, as he grew in years but not in stature, his parents withdrew more and more, relying on a nanny to care for this sickly child. The joy and love that other children relished was absent. Magic played no part in his young life: fantasy had little place. All of this was rather bad luck for Timothy. Growing up in Wales was anything but easy with the cruel remarks other school kids would make, calling him 'Timmy Midget – The Welsh Dwarf'.

In the ensuing years, he grew hardly any taller and the admiration that had been bestowed upon him as a young child turned to amazed inquisitiveness. He was a curiosity, some even used the word 'freak', thinking he didn't understand. Increasingly he became more self-reliant and independent. He had to, turning from the world that had turned from him. Lessons at home ensured his circle of friends was restricted to the neighbourhood lads who, over time, accepted him as he was. His tutor told him he was special and tried hard to encourage him to think of himself in that way. Life certainly taught him that he was different and, for some that he would encounter, too different. Luckily for him this did little to undermine him: his intellect and self-belief was too great for that. Now he became known as a 'Little Person' and that was fine by him.

One friend had loyally remained at his side throughout. Chas, a courageous cowboy, sewn and stuffed and equally small, had been his constant companion since his early nursery days. But for Timothy, Chas was more than a secret friend and had become his confidant, his soul-mate. No one else shared the same relationship with him that Chas did. Timothy could talk to him about anything, knowing it would go no further. Chas's replies made a lot of sense and, usually, were just what Timothy was thinking.

Timothy was told that his short stature was not a result of any particular disease or medical problem. Equally he didn't suffer from disproportionality: each of his body parts was the right size relative to the other, just smaller – well, that's what Stella assured him. It was impossible, however, not to notice that his legs were bowed more than most people's. Timothy would joke that it was as if the bones in his legs didn't know they were meant to be short and had started growing sideways, then finally got back together.

Living on his own in his simple home on wheels, Timothy surrounded himself with the trappings of his unusual life. Propped upon a faded eiderdown on a bunk in the corner of his caravan sat Chas, surveying their home. Perched either side of Timothy's long-standing friend were the tools of his trade, the glove puppets of Punch and Judy. For Timothy, 'Professor Lorenzo's Punch and Judy Show' had been his passion and his life. The archaic, hunchback Punch with his large, ruddy, hooked nose was clothed in a bright, scarlet jester's tunic and gold, tasselled hat. He sat ominously grasping the large wooden stick with which Timothy would have him strike Judy, their baby, the hungry crocodile and the officious policeman. Any puppet that came within reach was a potential and worthy victim.

Cuddled close beside Chas was Judy; dear old long-suffering Judy in her white pinafore dress, blue blouse and yellow mop-cap. In the hands of Timothy, Judy would be the focus of Punch's outrageous and often violent attention, much to Punch's gleeful satisfaction.

Timothy loved how he could become anyone but himself. The extravagant and exaggerated performance transported him and his audience to a world in which anything went: a world of slapstick and mayhem, the bizarre and the grotesque. Professor Lorenzo, or as Timothy knew him George, would drag around with the red-and-white striped booth a large box for Timothy to stand on, so he had a fighting chance of grappling with the performance. As Punch and his fellow performers captivated the audiences that Lorenzo had corralled before the gaily-decorated booth, collecting their money as he went, Timothy would set about enthralling and taunting the crowd with the puppets' antics and tricks.

On the occasions when spiteful children mocked Timothy about his height, George would console him by explaining that history told of 'Little Men' like himself, who had achieved greatness: Alexander the Great, Napoleon and the more interesting character, Attila the Hun. As far as Timothy was concerned, it did the trick.

Together they had travelled the resorts and market towns of southern England, encouraged by the riotous crowds and the wonderful roving lifestyle. That was until George had a heart attack.

Stuffed above the beams in Timothy's van was stored the discarded canvas booth, a sign of times past. Next to the wrought-iron cooking stove and stack of bleached-dry driftwood sat Timothy's old box, the one he would stand on, filled with what he regarded as his treasures. Amongst the other tired glove puppets was entwined a string of prop sausages and, staring at them intently, the hungry crocodile. Of course he might have been searching for the baby, as crocodiles do, muttering to himself, "Where's the baby?" To which Punch would have replied, "That's the way to do it!"

On a shelf above the box, well out of reach of the puppets, sat Timothy's swizzle, its squawky voice long since silent.

Timothy missed old George, the shouts from the audience, their laughter and their screams. Above all he missed their applause and adulation. It had been a good life and, who knew, maybe one day, a life to which he would return.

Chapter 6

Beyond Timothy's pied-à-terre, at the far eastern end of the long shore stood the foreboding Listening Station, dominating the wilderness on the very edge of the coastline. Ominous grey, concrete buildings, their perfect proportions following the golden ratio of 40 feet long by 24¾ feet wide and 12 feet high, were arranged in a matrix. There were a dozen or more, each completely encircled by sand banks 20 feet high. Interconnecting tunnels penetrated these banks, integrating the individual blocks into a huge commanding complex. A small compound of huts on its periphery strategically guarded access to this isolated, experimental centre and all that was secret within.

Close by, upon the grassy dunes backing the shingle beach, stood three massive, weather-beaten reflectors. Fashioned from concrete, two appeared as dishes, their faces looking to the sky: one about 30 feet across and round, the other oval. A wall, 26 feet in height and curving for its entire length of 200 feet, faced directly out to sea, staring at the horizon. In concert with the surrounding, desolate landscape, these military structures brought a haunting sense of bare ugliness, an overbearing menace.

Few knew what went on here: most didn't care. The shroud of secrecy that overshadowed this dark place was just another example of the strange goings-on in these parts. Movements of trucks and tanks, the build-up of vast numbers of troops, many not from around here, the rumoured construction of harbours and floating platforms further along the coast; all went largely unnoticed by the people of Doon. For the Dooners, World War Two had largely passed by this sleepy little fishing village, or so it seemed for the moment. Archie had once seen what he thought was a British Navy frigate way off-shore, whereas Seth, high up in his lighthouse, had never considered that the threat of attacks from France had passed, certain that without his vigilance, all Britain would be lost.

For many in the village these reflectors appeared as monstrous eyesores and, over the years, these acoustic mirrors detected inbound invading aircraft and became known as the Giant Ears. Carl, one of the twin brothers living on the beach, knew better. He had worked at the Station for seven years before being retired through ill health, a term which covered a multitude of disorders, including his mental breakdown. He had known that absolute secrecy had to be maintained. It was vital and that had proved a great burden of responsibility for him, particularly when combined with the strains involved in a project of such magnitude.

Local folk had not appreciated the impact this had had on his life, but Bernard, his twin, knew full well its effect and the sacrifices he in particular had to make for his brother. Living with a man on the brink of madness, for that was what Carl was, brought with it challenges that any lesser mortal would have found too much. Carl had developed an appetite for the bizarre, a remorseless cunning that proved wearing, an impulsiveness that was unsettling and, above all, the inhabitation of a world within which no one else dwelt.

There was a time when the two brothers were so very close, fully committed and beholden to the other. Advancing years, changing personalities and Carl's deteriorating health had dramatically changed all that, although Bernard still felt a deep sense of responsibility and caring for his increasingly confused twin. But Carl didn't see it that way: for him Bernard was interfering and overbearing, continually frustrating and disrupting his plans.

The fisherman's shack they inhabited stood erect with stripes of seasoned brown rust trickling down its rippling, tin-sheet roof. Spongy leeks, sedums and mosses clustered and vegetated in its gutters; a timber water butt oozed, overflowing with the rain that these parts were over-blessed with. The shack's lap-planked walls, garishly painted in a vile green, were blistering and cracking. Dislocated, bare wood-shutters hung on the window frames, dejected and discarded, and the front door groaned at its opening. Inside, a musty smell lingered in the dingy old dwelling which seemed to overflow with misery and anguish. It never used to, but now everything was different.

Bernard, the elder by forty minutes, chose to spend his time outside tending what had become a unique and all-consuming garden, which in itself was fortuitous, because Carl never left the shack. Sleeping in separate parts of the hovel, they had little to do with each other. That again had been something that had changed just after Carl started to become weird. Bernard wished their older brother Anton was still alive and here: he would have known how best to handle things. He would have reminded them of how things used to be.

"I can recall as if only yesterday, when the three of us children would while away hours pretending to be knights, guarding our grand home, our castle, from marauders. It was an exceedingly happy time. Mayta had created for us all a house overflowing with love, and

Puppa, a home where we could all feel safe. They both had a real pride in us boys. As the years added to our lives we three grew even closer, sharing everything, enjoying everything: until that day.

"It seemed a day like any other; we were to play in the yard, charging about on our pretend horses as once again we chivalrously fought off the imaginary peasants who were invading our secret kingdom. Ever since we were small, an understanding existed that the yard was the extent of our world. But on this day, that was to change. The butcher's delivery lad had called early on his errands, as each Tuesday and Friday he would. This day his departing was interrupted by a torrential downpour from the heavens. Usually he would close the gates behind him with his going, as Mayta had instructed, but whether it was the deluge, or an urgency to finish his round, the gates were left unlatched. In spite of our parents' endeavours to protect us, for us this was an offer too great to ignore, a temptation not to be resisted."

Anton would have paused and coughed, still suffering from the chest problems of his youth, before he would have continued his chronicle.

"Our game took on a new spirit of adventure, a new realm of challenge: to go outside our castle walls and, as noblemen, to lead a crusade, seeking out those foreign raiders who threatened our world.

"For much of the summer the earth road was a dusty track; clouds of fine grit and sand would rise into the air with each passing horse and cart. On this day, however, it had become a hideous, muddy-brown river, a great, new world for us boys to discover. Part of the thrill of such an excursion was knowing we were not meant to be doing this: the other was being unsure if we would ever be discovered! Even now I can still hear, echoing in my head, the deafening noise of the incessant rain pounding on the road.

"I never saw the cart and certainly didn't hear it. Appearing as if from nowhere, the wooden chassis seemed to loom above me. The horse lurched to one side, rearing, confused and scared, as a heavy, steel-rimmed wheel rolled over my body, snapping my ribs and crushing the very life from me. It was all over so quickly for me, but it would never be over for my family. The years that followed did little to bring comfort to them and, for my two remaining brothers Bernard and Carl, their reliance on each other grew even stronger."

Looking down now on his brothers from above as he did meant he heard their hostile words to each other and could see how they had grown to dislike one another. It saddened him, so much so that his heart was crushed for a second time. For years their mother had held the family together, but with her passing, a pillar of female strength was now missing. No other woman had played such a part in their lives and their insular existence had become increasingly isolating for them both. Carl hadn't noticed the change as he withdrew into his own world. Bernard, at one time, would have welcomed a relationship with a woman but the opportunity never seemed to arise and now he had become totally absorbed in his garden.

From under his wide-brimmed Panama hat, Bernard was busily tending his garden, telling each plant individually precisely how well it was doing. He chuckled to himself and then coughed, a dry cough, whilst irrigating the roots of each plant in turn, determined that the vegetables and few precious flowers were going to be given the chance of survival for yet another day. Resting from his early exertions, he yawned, settled on a low, rustic bench he'd made the previous year from collected driftwood, and gathered his thoughts. He nodded in deep satisfaction at the way in which the meandering, pebble path, its edges determined by a band of broken mussel shells, weaved its way through the plot. Strings of bone-dry kelp hung draped over the pallet fence he had erected to act as a windbreak and boundary to his domain. The seaweed's stiff, black tentacles, laden with salt crystals, sparkled in the sunlight as if diamond-encrusted. On a warm day the pungent odour of tar, used to coat the pallets, hung in the air. Bernard relished the smell of tar; it delighted his senses and reassured him that the evil decay of wood rot would be held at bay for another winter.

The garden was furnished with various flotsam and jetsam; multifarious ropes weaved patterns of many colours between driftwood of all shapes and sizes that struck stark, sculptural images amongst the shell beds and decaying, corroded ironware. Weird edifices, constructed from that which the sea and land had given up, poised menacingly, as if from some Orwellian fantasy. All that was discarded, all that was broken and worthless to others played its part within Bernard's creation. A crudely styled weathervane formed from flattened tin, orange twine and waxed string signalled the source of the weather.

Come calm or gale, fog or shine, rain or drought, Bernard would labour in his garden regardless of the prevailing conditions. To him this remote, peaceful place was staggeringly beautiful and magical, a beachcomber's paradise, a revelation. Tides toyed with the shingle, causing shelves and ridges to retreat and advance again and again, endlessly confused. A series of straggling strandlines along the beach marked the change in tides from springs to neaps, where seaweed of all shapes and colours – green, red, brown and black

– were heaped together in their new home. Sand flies and beetles feasted among the entangled weed. Tiny, porcelain-white crabs that scavenged for rotting carrion, lengths of bleached rope, odd worn-out shoes, sodden fish crates: all manner of things found their way here. Bernard had even found skeletal remnants of creatures that once inhabited these wild seas and skies, for this was Bernard's treasure trove: all that he wanted, all that he needed for his garden, came to him this way. This was his sanctuary, his escape from all that troubled him and, above all, Carl.

The room that Carl occupied had a strange sombreness about it. A grim feeling of misery seemed to linger, a chilling eeriness shrouded by the darkness that cloaked this place. Mysteriously appearing, as if from a past world, the room was a living memory for Carl: memories that had now been tarnished by time. Cabinets, shelves, machines and contraptions pressed tightly upon the room's yawning space. This was the largest room in the shack, but one would never suspect as much from a cursory glance. It appeared as if all the clutter of the world was gathered in this one place.

There were weighty tomes, used for reference and holding things down. Lightweight novels adapted to level tables and cabinets. Notepads on which to scribble and scrawl, art books in which to sketch and plan, account books to detail costings and schedules, and graph paper to envisage designs upon. Music score sheets were ideal for him to colour and construct patterns on, but, most importantly of all, crossword books were meticulously and religiously completed. Thumbed sheets of lovingly-crafted prose were jammed in the jaws of an archaic, black, steel typewriter, proudly bearing the badge of 'Underwood'. A blackboard, barely visible in this dim light, was crammed with white, chalked lists and mathematical formulae, as well as a bulbous drawing of a gigantic pig, a pretty realistic likeness it must be said. Highly technical plans and sectional drawings of dishes and parabolic reflectors were taped over the few windows that adorned his domain, their dyeline print now almost entirely faded. Toilet rolls had been unravelled and the paper draped high, like streamers, along the walls with words painted in bold, red characters about its length – 'tools', 'glue', 'boots', 'WIRE', 'screws', 'food', 'wood', 'oil', 'RUBBISH', and so it went on. Newspapers, neatly folded and stacked in piles that almost touched the ceiling, were balanced along one wall: 7,349 of them at the last count. Precariously perched on top of a pile, and proudly standing on one orange, webbed foot, was a rather shabby, stuffed swan, its once white plumage now thickly coated in grimy dust. Upon the other piles, and any bare wall space, were black-and-white and sepia photographs of people he'd known: colleagues he'd worked with at the Listening Station and various friends and family members. One such photograph included his brother Bernard, but Carl had painted a big, red cross over his face.

Carl, emotional, frustrated, tiresome, intolerant and fat, grimaced. Confined, not so much by the room itself, but by all its clutter, he busied himself searching for something, his form casting wild and restless shadows about the room. The harder he strained to look for whatever it was, the more it evaded him. It must have been hidden in the darkest and most secret of places. Repeatedly Carl would hide his most important secrets for fear they might be revealed, disclosed to another. Whilst sprawled across the floor, agitatedly moving bottles and jars of medical specimens, he started to mumble to himself; a sliver of saliva ran silently down from his mouth, rolling off his dirty clothes as it descended and finally found its way to an old, shabby rug on the floor.

Carl's wide, puckered lips pursed shut, instantly causing his cheeks to suck in like some deflated tyre. His chin dimpled and an elongated mole, reddish-brown in colour, wobbled at the edge of his mouth. His hazel eyes stared from deep within their sockets, emphasising his craziness which was perpetuated in the wiry, bushy hair skirting his balding head. Over time his hair had been allowed to run riot and covered his ears and the collar of his grey, tweed jacket. An unruly, red bow tie, decorated with white dots, waved from his frayed shirt collar, looking grand had it not been for the stains it bore.

A feverishness pulsed through Carl's veins that was all consuming as he continued to search through the fifteen tons of junk; he had an idea in his head and he wouldn't let it go. Carl was now incapable of appreciating that some ideas were best left as precisely that.

Bernard straightened his arched back, curved by his seventy-odd years. His chubby face beamed as he perused the distant scene before him. Along the beach a marooned boat lay on its side, dragged to its resting place before the old winch hut. A rusting lorry engine propped shut the hut's driftwood door; however, gaping lapwood wall panels and missing corrugated roof sheets ensured ferocious, salt winds could still whistle throughout the hut, creating a 'concert of the elements' as he would excitingly call it. An ancient, steel chain, half submerged under shingle, curled its way like a menacing snake about the beach and nearly reached his garden.

Both the brothers were a dying breed.

Chapter 7

Dilly's face shone and her blue eyes sparkled with delight. The late afternoon sunlight glowed golden in her long, blonde hair which touched her shoulders. Kneeling by the tide line the surf washed between her toes. She looked up and, noticing him standing over her, "You're not from about here are you?" she said, standing up to face him. In an accent she couldn't quite place, he shared that his homeland was Norway, but now he was stopping in one of the old shacks. She looked upon this mystical man in wonder. A broad smile filled his face. She had seen him on her beach just the once before but was never going to forget him.

"What are doing here?" she implored.

His answer came confidently and swiftly, "I'm a solitary adventurer."

She said nothing, but her body told all he needed to know.

"And you?" his voice was soft and caring. "Why are you here?"

She could stand the pain no longer, embarrassed in case he should notice: a sense of foolishness washed through her. Dilly moved from him and then, in a faltering voice, told him she must go. He called after this beautiful, young woman as she ran across the beach, "What are you called?"

Without stopping, without turning, her voice was heard to carry on the faint breeze, "Dilly . . . I am Dilly."

He rarely ventured to this end of the beach, but today he wanted to reconnoitre the lighthouse. The Station was where his real interest lay, however: there was something about the huge, dish structures that fascinated him. For hours on end he would sit atop the dunes sketching, detailing the terrain and coastline, mapping the Listening Station complex and its giant ears, annotating his work with copious notes. Few knew anything of him for he chose to keep himself to himself. Blending into the background as he did, locals rarely noticed his comings and goings and that was how he liked it.

Bernard was unsure of exactly when the young man had arrived: he just appeared. An oil lamp had flickered in the window of the shack one night, the first signs of life since the passing of Charlie. Charlie, the old marshman whose hut it had been, had spent his life wandering the acres of coastal, salt marshland. The 'Wild Gooseman', as he became known, was familiar with the challenging tides that threatened this land, flooding vast swathes of it, and the behaviour of the migrating wildfowl that he hunted from sun-up to sundown. Bernard could remember old Charlie bemoaning on many occasions that to be as cold as he was, you had to be dead, and now, after that tragic accident on the marshes, he was. The storm seas played cruel tricks on these hidden mires, inundating and ever moving the cursed marshlands. On wild days the restless wind whipped up waves which pounded and roared onto the beach: even on calm days, when barely a ripple broke the surface, vast waters rolled beneath the surface, shifting the pebbles on the sea's shore.

A flock of sea swallows, patrolling the water's edge, was disturbed. Their alarm call went out, "Kee-aah", and they rose nervously into the air like a languid cloud, twisting from side to side as they climbed.

Once again a meagre plume of smoke poked above the stack pot of Charlie's old shack and weaved its path skywards into the sunset.

Chapter 8

It was said that when it was high water and all the village was asleep, crabs crawled along the seafront and knocked on the cottage doors, but by the time their residents got the doors open, they'd gone. Probably they'd scurried up Maid's End Lane to the church to dig yet another grave.

One grave that they didn't dig was that of Mary Bells. Local folklore had it that back in the sixteenth century, a fair, young maiden, by the name of Mary Bells, was jilted by her lover on their wedding day. As she waited on the church threshold, the news of him fleeing with another came to her, whereupon she broke down, distraught, vowing to end her life. That evening, Mary, desperate, took herself up the lane to where the three, lone trees stand firm upon the crest above the churchyard and, casting a rope over a high bough of the middle of the three trees, hanged herself. It was told that on that ill-fated day each August, when her restless soul yearned to find peace, her ghost prowled the church and graveyard of Doon, crying and pining for her lost love.

But she would not be the only young woman who ever made her way up Maid's End Lane late at night.

"Come in the dark, don't use a light," implored Tobias Pritchard, the farm lad of dear Molly Lund. That night The Ship had let Molly go early from her barmaid duties, on account of her feeling poorly.

"Why?" Molly pressed Tobias.

"We must not be seen in the graveyard, you and me, alone together."

And there he waited for her in the mellow moonlight. In time she appeared, dazzling in her scarlet dress, weaving through the maze of watchful trees, dilapidated gravestones, twisted gorse and brambles and the damp, mossy mounds, to meet her lover, and there they lay. The only stirring that night within the graveyard was the rustle of herbage, but not the herbage whose stems were soft, that died after their flowering. No, this was the herbage that was deep-rooted on the chin of Tobias Pritchard: once butcher's boy, twice removed from Reverend Dunbar's choir and now guardian of Colonel Grossett's prized pigs. His stamina was unequalled in the village, as Molly was only too aware! They lay where Molly had often lain on these clear evenings, content beneath the stars, grunting, just like the Colonel's pigs. She felt at one with him as together they rolled on the damp grass.

The heavens turned dark. Blackened clouds veiled the moon and a distant rumble announced an approaching storm. Rain began to drip from the branches that formed an umbrella over them; then it poured, pounding down, soaking everything. Feverish with wild passion they devoured the love of each other. A fork of yellow lightning pierced the electric air, its finger with a crack-like whip overhead, streaked to earth time and time again. The tortuous storm grumbled and groaned, shaking the sky and the very ground where they lay. This awesome power, the maelstrom, the turmoil, the climax of forces was no match for the energy Tobias and Molly were unleashing below. For now they too had climaxed. There was nowhere else for them to go in their quest to find love on this hallowed turf.

For years Doon was almost totally cut off from the outside world. The occasional truck with goods would visit, making its way to the small community spread across this desolate landscape, buffeted by the fierce winds coming from every which way, strong enough to waken the dead. Negotiating the winding track as it weaved its way across the wasteland between the shifting mires was never easy. And then there was the fog, which in a moment would close in, seemingly denser than ever. Nothing was ever the same here, nothing ever easy. This was the land that folklore called 'The Isle in the Clouds'. Travellers, bearing their loads, would come and go along the narrow, sunken, harrowed paths, following the sheep tracks, their feet treading new trails through the invading nettles and briars across this dangerous land criss-crossed with water courses.

Then with the building of the road, everything changed. Every couple of days the fish-man would visit in his pick-up, delivering supplies and buying fish to be transported by train to the merchants Trough and Noggin at Billingsgate Market. That was in the days when many crews fished these waters for cod, plaice, Dover sole, crabs and turbot. But that was in seasons long gone and, for many, the gruelling life had proved too much for their advancing years and boats had been hauled ashore for the last time to die and rot. Yet for Archie's catch, the fish-man still came. He was a weak, sickly looking character: it might have been that he had spent too long around fish, who knows. Nevertheless he not only smelt but looked like them. His fine hair was as silver as a sea bass, his snout as long and pointed as a sturgeon's and his body as thin as a sand eel. All in all he was no more appealing than a John Dory and as slimy as a sea slug! This was the fish-man who would end his day in the bar of the local hostelry, The Ship. This night, however, the talk would be anything but easy, for the fish-man had spoken of war.

"War?" scoffed a local.

"Yes, war," countered the fish-man, "the Nazis are sweeping through Europe bringing death and destruction. Don't you read the news?"

"As long as they stay put over there," an old boatman insisted as he rose in an ungainly fashion. Wobbling from side to side he continued, "And don't come bothering us." Reaching the bar he called, "Two more pints, Molly my dear."

The fish-man piped up again, "Our world's going mad."

As Molly pulled another pint, she looked up and innocently asked, "Who's going mad?"

"The world!" the fish-man shouted. "Men are dying in their thousands, fighting for peace and freedom."

"Well, I've not noticed that hereabouts," the boatman mumbled scornfully as he settled on his bench in the corner of the bar. "It's a lot of fuss for naught," he concluded, trying to bring the conversation to an end.

"Young British lads will never see their families again," the fish-man continued, not wanting to be ignored so easily.

"Is that so?" came from someone in the bar, but it was unclear from whom.

Brown billows of smoke drifted from the briars of the men seated in the bar and swirled about, clinging, hanging, lingering heavily above their heads. Molly was next to contribute.

"Aye, Mavis was saying that her sister Audrey's boy, in the RAF, 'twas missing, he'd be only nineteen. She said the lad 'twas only after a bit of adventure. 'Tis a shameless sin all because of this Adolf fellow!"

"Damn murderer should be shot," came the unknown voice again.

In a feeble attempt to bring some urgency to the matter, the fish-man declared that he was ready to be called up to fight. One old boy swore of how on perfectly still evenings you could sometimes hear, coming over the marshes, the ghostly roar of the engines of a German bomber that had been shot down. The ever hungry marsh had swallowed it and its crew whole, never to give them up.

Over the ensuing thirty minutes, little by little, bit by bit, the subject was gradually changed and the tension dispersed; but for the fish-man the frustration and futility of it all ate away at him, making him bitter that here was a community which knew and cared little for the countless cruelties of war.

An ancient seafarer, full of good intentions, struck up a shanty, and all, many the worse for beer, joined in the chorus:

> "The evening red and morning grey
> are sure signs of no finer day,
> but the evening grey and the morning red,
> makes the sailor shake his sullen head.
> He shakes his sullen head."

Uniting, if not the nation then certainly those in the bar, the rhythmical recitations, witticisms and tales were rehearsed late into that night.

Chapter 9

Rarely did Percy Pough frequent the local. Instead he would while away the evenings tending his beloved budgerigars, much to the annoyance of his overbearing wife Doris, who had little time for his long-standing passion. In fact, Doris would not have been unhappy at all if all the birds were to die: equally Percy would not have been unhappy if the same fate were to befall Doris. Prune-faced, this red-haired woman would glare at him across the kitchen table with her widely-spaced eyes that fixed him through her thick glasses, appearing as large red beetroots, an image perpetually burnt into Percy's brain.

Behind the General Stores at the top of their garden sat Percy's shed. Inside, row upon row of cages lined the shelves Percy had erected. In each cage sat a solitary budgerigar, some forlorn and friendless, but most of them contentedly settled upon their perches, puffing up and showing off their plumage or pecking in the sand tray looking for seed. Eighty-four of them lived and chirped at the end of his garden, in a shed that Doris daren't visit and where no-one else was welcome. Here birds of every shade, colour and pattern occupied his aviary; albinos, cinnamons, sky blues and opalines, all champions-in-the-making and a result of years of careful breeding. Percy's budgies were the best of the best. The bloodlines were second to none, so it was imperative that both the breeding aviary and each individual cage was comprehensively alarmed. They were wired back to his bedroom. He knew full well other fanciers and breeders would rip his right arm off to get hold of his breeding stock.

Such achievement had not come easily: it had taken hard work and concerted endeavour on his part and certainly was not achieved on a wing and a prayer! The right balance of the bird was the key: its deportment from head to body. Not everyone could tell a perfect breeding bird from one that was a run-of-the-mill, but Percy could. It was a knack – and he had it.

Percy would endlessly scour the beach searching for pearl-white cuttlefish: seed would be begged, borrowed or stolen when Doris couldn't get it from the wholesalers. If supplies were short he'd scrounge gleanings from the nearby threshing machines and make do. The little wall space that was left in his shed was adorned with prize rosettes of every colour from every competition. For him this was a serious business. His cherished trophies were safely tucked away under the bed in their cottage. Doris said there was no way she was having them cluttering up the place and, after all, they were harbingers of dust.

At the age of seven he had started out on this journey following the example of his late uncle who regarded himself as just a feather fancier. But for Percy, from the first moment he had won a junior championship, he was hooked and now he was a fanatic.

Percy's champion and twice 'Best of Show' was an exquisite grey-green male with fluffy, yellow head-feathers, reminiscent of a wispy dandelion, which went by the grand name of Percy's Princely Pride the Third. But for Percy, the real acknowledgement of his achievement was when he was asked to become the secretary of the Budgerigar Society.

No longer was it an avian hobby that attracted him. It was his life and nothing else mattered, not even Doris. As far as Doris was concerned, that was fine as the store was her world. Whereas others would find pricing, shelf stacking, arranging window displays and dealing with irritating, if not flirtatious, commercial travellers boring, Doris loved it. Even the annual stock-taking held a magic for her. Most of all though, she loved and revelled in the gossip and there was no shortage of that. The ladies of Doon would frequent her store on the feeblest of excuses, perhaps stocking up their larders with no more than one or two items, a can of beans or some corned beef; but the real attraction was catching up on all the village news. The disasters and delights, the affections and affairs, all was fair game when it came to disseminating the gospel of Doon. Modesty and confidentiality had no place. For between the dusty, musty shelves and stacks of mops, matches, potatoes, suet, tinned meat, fish, spam, dried milk, powdered egg, sugar, tea, cocoa, buckets, bleach and soap, revelations were made and secrets exposed, usually next to dishes of pig's feet jelly, arranged on the counter top and freshly made from Colonel Gossett's prized pigs. As a matter of fact, it was like any normal village shop, except for Doris, who'd stand by the cash drawer conducting and orchestrating proceedings. In these times of wartime austerity Doris would religiously and even-handedly adopt the policy of rationing everything with the exclusion of gossip!

Miss Pippa McWalters, schoolmistress of this parish, employee of the revered Education Authority and staunch supporter and admirer of the reverend Thomas Dunbar, wouldn't have dreamt of letting a bad word cross her lips. Such exemplary behaviour, however, never crossed the minds of Ivy Oliver, the ever-nosey Margie Richards, Olive Smart and, on occasions, Freddie and Fergus, two old boys who still loved a jaw. There was no shortage of material, for everyone was related to everyone else somewhere along the line. Seth, the lighthouse keeper rarely darkened the door of Doris's emporium, not wishing to leave his tower and telescope unattended. Buying his family's provisions fell to Dilly. Dilly never spent a moment speaking ill of others and Doris had a deep affection for her as everyone did. She was adored by the old men in their twilight years, respected by the women for the way she dedicated herself to her father, and loved by the mischievous children that played and ran riot around the village.

Dilly loved being young and never wanted to grow any older. She felt truly alive, free to indulge her passion for life and, drowning in her dreams, she wanted nothing to change.

Once again the young man came upon Dilly on the beach. She hadn't noticed him, sitting as she was on a sun-bleached trunk of driftwood, reading intently. He trod softly, determined not to disturb her, just watching and gazing at this young woman to whom he had only briefly spoken. Her sky-blue, cotton dress seemed to reflect the very vibrancy of the sea, its folds and creases as if waves and ripples. A light tan straw hat shaded her face which looked down, studying, reading her letter. Something interrupted her concentration and she glanced up; a lone oyster catcher lifted lightly from the shore and made for the pearly light of the distant horizon on its own journey of discovery, or so she imagined to herself.

Axel believed she'd noticed him and spoke. Her spirit lifted as he shared with her how he had fallen in love with the raw beauty of this place, its isolation, and how it reminded him of home. They chatted idly as they strolled along the beach below the dunes. Little by little, feeling more confident in his company, she talked of her childhood and he recalled his upbringing amid the western fjords of Norway.

Wandering the beach together they explored the glistening seaweed, newly stranded and hiding a multitude of mysteries. The bulbous tentacles of bladder wrack were woven amongst heaps of green and brown weed, sheltering scavenging sand hoppers, dead razor shells and tiny, agitated crabs that scurried this way and that. Dilly, picking up a pale-coloured purse-like object explained to Axel it was the egg case of a dogfish. This fish was the scourge of local fishermen, eating their catch before it was landed. Her mother used to call it a mermaid's purse. The purse attached to the kelp in the deeper water and, having endured the worst of the winter storms, grew throughout the summer. By late autumn it was nearly ready to hatch. As the sun's light weakened at the ending of the year, the kelp forest died, rotting away to nothing and a dogfish emerged, its long tail just like that of a mermaid.

Over the ensuing days Axel and Dilly spent hour after hour taking pleasure in being in each other's company, learning of the other's ways and desires, delights and loves, considering the ordinary and extraordinary. He found her beguiling. They sat in the sea and amongst the sand grasses, surrounded by a profusion of flowers and fragrance, resting in the peace of one another's company.

"Another busy day?" inquired Kennie Smart of Doris Pough as she handed him his weekly indulgence of a slim pack of pipe tobacco.

"Aye," she offered, and no more, encouraging his departure, conscious of the time the store clock was telling. "Be away with you," she uttered under her breath, "and don't drink too much."

She ushered him out onto the seafront. Doris slammed the door behind him, locking and bolting it as she closed the store for another day. Doris checked the windows were shut, latched up the counter flap, but just as she was about to head through the rear door to her cottage, a tapping on the window stopped her. Kennie Smart was back, rapping on the glass and pointing to the door. The sign on the door announced to the whole world that she was still open. She acknowledged Kennie's trouble and with a flip, the white card was turned, then swung from side to side bouncing against the pane. Closed!

"Night," she cried to him, a farewell sufficiently loud enough for him to hear outside. The lock on the rear door no longer clicked confidently into place as Doris turned the well-worn key. The years of service had taken their toll.

So once again the village store had had its day and so too had Doris Pough.

Molly Lund, meanwhile, was restocking The Ship with bottles and polishing the tankards ready for another heavy night. Stella was preparing a thick, stinking mackerel and cabbage stew for Archie, and Pippa McWalters, deep in thought once again, struggled to exact a plan for her lessons tomorrow. In the manse, Thomas Dunbar was enjoying a well-earned rest and a moment of peace having persuaded Precious to take a nap. Bernard had no such luck: Carl was as manic as ever, creating chaos in their little shack. Little Joshua, Harry, Gracie and Isabel, the youngest of the village children, had already started their night's dream journeys, and Percy Pough, well, he was busy tending to his budgies.

Next door, in Archie's garden, some plants were doing well, positively flourishing, whereas others were struggling, battling for light, space and nutrients. A few of them had become sickly and had eventually died and that, coincidentally, was how life would be for the folk of Doon.

High in his tower, buffeted by the weather, Seth sat commanding a view of the village and beyond. Straining his eyes, squinting, blinking and focusing through his telescope, his face wrinkled like a tortoise. Yet he saw nothing, only countryside, sea and sky. He had no worries for his dear Dilly, knowing that she spent her days on the beach. What he didn't know was that today it was with a stranger.

Chapter 10

One month to the day since he arrived in Doon and two weeks since he first met Dilly, Axel agonised over his circumstances.

Gone was his freedom and undoubtedly gone were those whom he once cherished. His world was a prison and he was its prisoner. Axel knew that his time with Dilly must soon end no matter how hard he yearned for it not to. Dilly was becoming more important to him than anyone or anything else. Life for him could never be the same, but he doubted he could tell her why he was in Doon. It was painful to see Axel in this way: a young man in such distress, fighting with himself. As Axel sat, he leant forward and rested his face in his hands, shaking his head and sobbing aloud. Here was a man who didn't know what to do, but what he did know was that he didn't want to hurt her.

They had met in secret on their beach many times and were closer now to each other than either had been to anyone ever before. They'd run into the sea together, the waves buffeting them as they fought to stay on their feet. Her laughter had filled the air and the excitement had thrilled her; these were the moments of dreams, the finest dreams she had ever known. To Axel, Dilly was beautiful, so pure and full of the joy of life. He so wished it could stay like this forever. For Dilly, here was the dawning of a new life. She hoped that this newfound love would never die, but that was hardly likely in this war. Who knew how long anyone might live? She lay beside him on the sand under the turquoise sky; she had never felt more alive, her whole body invigorated by the exquisite magic of this moment. She found it impossible to understand how this had happened and to imagine where it would end. If only time would stand still, preserving this instant forever. They hardly spoke, content to lie in one another's arms.

She sensed he was restless. He seemed unsettled. There was something she now found unnerving about him.

"What is it, what's wrong?"

It was clear he desperately wanted to answer her but something was holding him back, preventing him from sharing with her what he so much wanted to.

"I need to talk to you, but I'm afraid I don't know where to begin or how to tell you."

Axel looked at her, uncertain of how she would react; Dilly, expectant and fearful of what he had to share, sat up and repeated, "What is it?"

Pleading he answered her, "Please, please don't stop me until I've told you all." Clutching her hand tightly, he leant forward and kissed her lightly on the cheek,

"I must tell you," Axel admitted, not wishing to hurt her but knowing full well if there was to be any future for them together, he had no choice. "I was a fool to think I could keep it from you. I never thought I would find someone and it would come to this. They said once I had sent them the information my family would be safe and I could return to Norway, but they say now they need more from me and I realise this will never be over."

"Who?"

"I no longer believe they will keep their promise to me and release my parents and sisters. I must have been a fool to ever think I could trust their word."

"Who are they?" she persisted.

"The Germans! My homeland was not prepared for war. We were neutral as in the Great War but after Finland's surrender, Hitler's Nazis invaded my beloved Norway. They needed control of our coast to ship minerals and house their submarines. Their forces surged through the country until they reached Oslo. I lived with my family in a small, coastal township outside Stavanger, in southern Norway. The Luftwaffe landed near us and there were sea attacks close by on Bergen, and south in Kristiansand. They came in their thousands. Our airforce had obsolete aircraft. Our army, swelled with volunteers, tried to fight back in the mountains and valleys. Our coastal batteries proved useless to fend off their attacks and men even set to sea to fight in tiny whale boats, but it was no good. Everything looked dark: my beloved homeland was in the hands of the Germans.

"They called themselves the Masters of the World. Stormtroopers broke into the schools and beat up teachers, condemning many to hard labour in the freezing Arctic north. Children were brutalised. Our pastor was forbidden to preach and sent away. Massive rewards were offered for information about resistance fighters and, with the collaboration of a Norwegian informer, the Germans arrested my family.

"You must understand, Dilly, they were killing my countrymen, destroying our fishing boats, our livelihoods and homes. They were ruthless. In our town many were shot trying to escape by boat to England, others were starved of food. They told me they were preparing the way for their mighty Luftwaffe to wreak havoc on the RAF bomber bases, to halt the raids on their people. If I helped them they would guarantee the life of my parents and three sisters."

Dilly was stunned, speechless.

"I had little choice. If I did not do as they asked they would kill my family. I didn't trust them, but what else could I do? They knew the British were developing radar to detect their approaching aircraft as they flew across the English Channel from the occupied French airfields. Intelligence had identified the secret Listening Station here, but they needed to know exactly what it was and its capability. A German agent had secured a hut for me to stay in and a submarine landed me on the beach under the cover of darkness. I thought it would be easy and within the month I would return home. But then I met you!"

There was a long silence: neither spoke. Tears welled in Dilly's eyes as she stared out to sea. After several minutes' silence, Axel spoke,

"I am not going to carry on spying anymore." He paused briefly, then in a quiet voice declared, "I have never met anyone like you before and, whatever happens, I don't want to lose you."

An early morning start for Archie after the whitening of the sky brought blissful sailing conditions. There was a lot of luck in fishing and today they had been lucky. Many silver-streaked fish were no longer weaving, dancing and shimmering in the water, but lay as a good haul in the bottom of the *Lively Lady*. More than sufficient reward for a day's labour.

A few days before there had been a full moon. The tides were running high and the Boil was thick with fish rising to the surface. The sea was seething with hundreds of bubbles breaking the surface. Archie could smell the fish; they almost leapt into his arms. These were the days when Archie was convinced seafaring was in his blood. The love of the sea seemed second nature to him.

The shipping forecast had been right: fair winds and fair weather, not foul, thank God, no fight or flight battling the elements out at sea this morning. Close to Worlds End rocks, an hour from Doon, Billy had spotted the old timer in his dinghy, harvesting the plentiful lobsters from his pots and keep boxes. A wave was exchanged, reassurance that all was well with him as he pulled another marker float aboard. He too was having a fair catch. Today the oily mackerel were drawing the lobsters from their weedy holes. He'd soon have them in coal dust with their long blue-black claws tied and on their way to market.

Wheeling gulls had followed their homeward journey, screeching incessantly overhead, expectantly awaiting their feast. They slid up the timbers on to the foreshore. With a "halli-hup" the old timers heaved the baskets of long line up the beach. Already, by the time Archie had secured the boat and clambered up the beach, a group of stout old fishwives were busy beginning to bait up the six lines of two hundred or so hooks, a salt soaked mussel or whelk impaled onto each of the barbs.

Once back home, Archie took to his patch and raked up the seaweed deep over his tatties. One of his greatest annoyances was the unwillingness of vegetables to grow in orderly straight lines. Finally, Archie came in for his supper and, after his fill, retired to his bath a contented man. He lay soaking, dreaming of being at sea, a pirate captain on the high seas, battling the furious squalls, the heavy, driving rain, ropes straining, timbers creaking, the boat groaning, harpoon in his hand as he plundered and searched for treasure.

Stella, in her bedroom next door, dreamt she was Lady Hamilton, adorned in a fine silk dress, standing on the poop deck of some magnificent galleon next to the short-in-stature Admiral Lord Nelson, attired in grand regalia, commanding his fleet.

Archie, on one of those rare occasions when he could slump in the bath, enjoyed the soap suds which blanketed the now tepid water and bubbled up his nostrils. He breathed in, which caused him to choke, cough and spit the offending foam from his mouth. His trip of fantasy had ended abruptly and just in time to hear Stella chanting "Oh Timothy, my Lord" from her bed.

Having turned in early, Timothy was sleeping uneasily on his bunk in the caravan, perhaps sensing that a bombshell had just been dropped nearby in Stella's cottage.

Tobias Pritchard wobbled, teetered, rocked back and forth and tried to steady himself with an outstretched hand resting against the wall above the urinal. His throat felt parched in spite of seven pints in quick succession having been poured down it in the past hour. He released all his pent up fluid in one flood into the pan, or so he thought as it was hard to tell in this dim light and with his blurred vision. Rearranging himself for the outside world he entered the public bar of The Ship. A piercing shard of light from behind the bar penetrated painfully deep into his brain, to the very place where all pain is detected. He blinked, closed his eyes, rubbed his lids, then tried again to search for the barmaid. He was in pain. His head throbbed so hard it felt as if a percussionist was playing drum rolls on his brain, now loose and being buffeted in a whirlpool of beer. Pausing to steady himself again, he realised all was far from well and there was little hope of improvement. Feeling very ill, he convinced himself he wasn't drunk, but didn't really know what he was.

"What the hell," he thought as he started on his eighth pint, served by lovely, ravishing, busty Molly, who, clearly aroused, or so he thought, kept eyeing his trousers. Any ideas that she was having problems controlling her animal urges vanished when Freddie nudged him and, casting a glance downward, uttered, "Yer zip, me old lad." So it was on account of the keen eyes and good works of these two vigilant and sober Doon residents that another embarrassment was narrowly avoided!

One could be excused for believing all was well again, but no. Tobias stretched across the bar and hooked out an anaemic-looking jellied eel from a pickle bowl. Just as easily as the eel had slid down his throat, it came back up and disgorged itself onto the fine-grained, oak bar that Molly had so meticulously polished that very afternoon. Tobias looked pathetically at Molly through his glassy eyes, clearly experiencing great difficulty in focusing, discerning enough of her most impressive features as she lent across the bar to wipe it down.

"You're a bloody wonderful woman Molly!" He paused, mustered all the energy he could and, in a loud voice, announced for the entire world to hear, "Oh Molly my love, I want to eat you," then, after an unwelcome burst of wind, sufficient to wake the dead, promptly collapsed on the floor and passed out.

The church clock struck eleven. Dunbar was still busy with the final preparation of his sermon and burning the late night oil. Tomorrow he would once again throw open the doors of the Lord's House to all who would venture in to hear his words of wisdom. Usually only seven souls came, but that was not important: what was important was that they came with open hearts and listening ears ready to receive God's word, to set aside all weaknesses of the spirit and flesh. He set down his pen, laid his notes to one side and, stretching, yawned deeply. Having climbed the stairs and entered Precious's bedroom, he gave her a kiss on the forehead: she didn't stir. Each night, at bedtime, he would also give Miss Philippa McWalters a kiss – in his imagination. It seemed to please her and it certainly pleased him. What Thomas Dunbar didn't know was that as he was readying himself for bed, Pippa McWalters was doing exactly the same a quarter of a mile down the hill, in her cottage.

There seemed no hope for Thomas to find love again. He was reconciled to living the rest of his life alone.

Chapter 11

Any sensual memories of Precious had now faded with the passing of time, of much earlier times if they ever did truly exist.

Our minds play funny tricks on us, sweetening those painful moments and softening those harsher times. Thomas's life had developed into a continual round of strife and sufferance; he knew not how he had endured it. He remembered the time when his wife swallowed a plump, succulent gherkin, the size of a swollen thumb, which went down the wrong way, blocking her windpipe. This caused temporary loss of voice, interrupting her continual chatter and breathing. Then again there was the occasion, whilst striding out, her legs pumping away like pistons and jawing ten to the dozen, she lost her balance, slipped and unconsciousness ensued. This, however, was short-lived and her incessant chatter soon returned in earnest. All in all there had been few rays of hope over the past few months and Lady Luck was hardly smiling on Thomas.

In the doorway of the manse, silhouetted in its porch by the new day's dawn, Dunbar lifted his heels, rocked onto the balls of his feet and stretched. After several seconds of this physical joy, he returned to the ground but not until he had first slapped his left hand in his right palm behind his back. For added delight this was accompanied by an all-telling, "Haar." His thoughts on a Sunday, at this early hour, turned to his parishioners as they still slumbered their last hours of sleep, snoozing in tranquil happiness. A moment was spared for each of them in turn as he stood in contemplation; then, and only then, would he cast his attention to the service.

As always a little song came to him which he sang to himself in what could certainly not be described as a musical rendition, but then no one else could hear so it didn't really matter.

> "First evening comes, which drifts so quietly by,
> then soon the sun will brighten up the sky.
> The clouds will break, a bright new day awakes
> and everyone needs to be filled,
> with the Lord's new love, His message from above,
> God's word fulfilled.
>
> I await the dawn with a twinkle in my eye,
> outstretch my hand to those who pass on by.
> A hymn or two, one perhaps they knew
> so memories don't need to stand still.
> With the Lord's new love, a prayer to Him above,
> God's word fulfilled."

Thomas's verse was simple, yet innocently sincere.

"Here comes Miss McWalters cycling with her pinafore dress blowing in the wind," said someone about to enter the church for the service.

Dunbar's ears pricked up and his heart, aroused, beat faster, throbbing beneath his robes. The words of his opening hymn went through his head – "All things bright and beautiful" – and when it came to its singing in the service, Stella couldn't resist a smile at the second line, "All creatures great and small". Dunbar was tackling the Ten Commandments, one each week, and today's message was focused on adultery, or more precisely that you should not commit it. The years had demonstrated that Thomas was not a natural preacher being neither eloquent nor inspirational, but rather more a meanderer and this was borne out by a declining congregation. It must be said, however, that for those few present, the message was particularly pertinent and Thomas was no exception. Two more hymns followed: 'Guide me, O thou great Jehovah' and 'Father hear the prayer we offer' whilst the offering was collected – six-shillings-and-thruppence. The closing prayer was one Thomas would often share, old words but in a different order. "We pray for our fishermen as each day they risk their lives, battling the elements to bring us the bounties of the sea; our farmers who labour caring for livestock, tending the land to provide for us food; for the soldiers of our land who fight for our protection and future peace."

He concluded his petition with a parting word to his congregation, "We may think we know what tomorrow holds, but only God will determine what the morrow brings for each of us. If we believe in God we have no fears because we are assured of life eternal."

Doris Pough, her new shoes squeaking loudly as leather ones do on occasions, made a beeline for Dunbar as the congregation departed. His initial thought was that he had touched a nerve and was about to be taken to task.

"It's my Percy." Dunbar sighed in relief, uncertain, however, where this conversation was heading. "He's lost his birds!" And with that news Doris looked distraught. "He's not the same. I always had difficulty understanding him, his obsession with his budgies, but never realised how much they meant to him."

"My dear lady," Dunbar responded. "Your soul is in deep torment." She nodded, aware of his sentiment but seemingly oblivious to his words.

"I confess I've ignored him; I've let him go his own way and now there seems little hope." Dunbar consoled her sensitively, resting his hand on her trembling shoulder.

"A stream of love flows through all of us, Doris," he said choosing his moment to use her Christian name with great care, wanting to personalise his appeal. "We are but mortal beings afflicted by sin and our own weaknesses, but an inner strength, a radiance shines from within you, my dear." He squeezed her shoulder gently. "Love can overcome all things if you allow it to."

In a funny sort of way she appeared calmer, at peace with herself and, turning, she hurried off purposefully, assuring Dunbar that she would do all in her power to reconcile her relationship with Percy. Thomas called after her by way of encouragement, "Not only in your power my dear, but with the power of someone far greater," and with that they exchanged distant smiles.

Dunbar, considering her outburst, mused to himself "'Tis mystery all."

Last, but by no means least, to approach him was the lovely Miss McWalters.

"Oh my dear, dear Miss McWalters. Philippa, Pippa, how beautifully you sang; your voice lifts my soul to a higher place, it elevates my heart." She never knew quite how to respond to him when he spoke in such a way. Deep down inside she relished his compliments and treasured his encouragement. "You are music, and music is in your blood," and with that Dunbar clasped her hand on the pretext of thanking her sincerely for her harmonious vocal contribution, and Pippa positively glowed. Old Prince, having silently crept up on the couple, looked at them, his hang-dog expression begging for his regular morning constitutional. As Thomas led Pippa and Prince away to stroll the neighbouring lush, green farmlands on this glorious day, he shared with both a few words of Tennyson, "Ring out the coldness of our times. Ring in the peace to all mankind."

Pippa gazed on, starry eyed, and felt captivated. Prince looked up, cataract-eyed, released a brief bout of wind, and felt comfortable.

Miss McWalters was a sharp, intuitive woman of fortitude, of strong uncompromising principles and staunch morals: her childhood had taught her the ways of right and wrong. Her body lacked any great physical attractiveness and she believed now that time was too short to do anything dramatic about it, accepting that some things were beyond hope. School took its toll on her and term time would wear her down mercilessly, exhausting her physically and mentally, often reducing her to a feeble wreck. But she knew Thomas well understood, supporting her as he did on many a school day: in fact, she'd noticed, increasingly so over the recent months. It wasn't that the few children in her school were particularly naughty: they were just full of beans, a tad mischievous and certainly proficient in winding her up. When tiredness and irritation got the better of her, it proved more than she could cope with and tiredness was a big problem for Pippa, sleeping fitfully as she did. Playful chants such as those her children would sing in the playground filled her head,

"Seventy-one, seventy-two, oh I'll catch you and if I do,

seventy-eight, seventy-nine, hurry up for I'll be right behind, eighty-four and eighty-five, you'll be mine dead or alive,

ninety-two, ninety-three, I wonder, I wonder where you'll be,

one-hundred, one-hundred-and-one, one for luck; ready or not, here I come!"

As so often happens there was no one rational reason for her restless nights, but one nightmare returned time and time again to haunt her. It concerned the difficulty she had experienced in furnishing her cosy cottage, in particular getting her ornate brass bedstead into her bedroom. Repeatedly, in her tormented sleep, she would move the frame with great care between the furnishings and furniture of her little home. Any sense of achievement, alas, quickly vanquished. Whilst executing the mission she discovered the doorway into her room did not entertain the now seemingly gigantic structure. Even if it had, more problems probably awaited her, but she didn't think that far ahead. A clatter of metal, a squeak of casters and the double bed was on the move again, this time to the chimney. By now she had worked herself into a frenzy as she fought with linen and mattress: her armpits exuded the all-pervasive stench of perspiration, those nails she had so carefully trimmed then filed, snapped as if sounding a ten-gun salute to celebrate a royal occasion. Her torso curved and bent simultaneously as, persevering, she attempted to force the bed over the hearth and from the dark depths to escape up, up, up to? And so the night would pass, leaving Philippa McWalters dreaming fretfully and scheming about new and outrageous ways of transporting the generous bed to her eagerly-awaiting boudoir.

All of this proved beyond any shadow of doubt that there was more to Miss Philippa McWalters than initially met the eye, and the Very Reverend Thomas Dunbar was becoming increasingly aware of that and relished his discovery.

Bolt upright on the tired settee belonging to Doris Pough sat a gimlet-eyed, authoritative and official, thirty-something P.C. Doyle, vigilant in his duties as ever. It had taken him but a short while to make his journey by bike from the town lock-up, along the highways, byways and pathways to Doon, in search of the truth. His quest throughout the county in the name of law and order ensured his physique remained slim and muscular, which was in complete contrast to the agitated man facing him across the room. Doyle's detection skills were second-to-none and it was no secret that such talent ran in his family. His father had been a policeman in the local force and, hopeful that his only son would follow in his footsteps, he named him Conan after an author he both admired and avidly read.

A short, squat man sat in an armchair opposite; his badly cut, black, greasy hair lay thick on his head. Sickly-looking and podgy from an over indulgence of fatty foods, Percy Pough looked distraught. Doyle tried to appear concerned,

"So what exactly happened, Percy?"

Percy, preoccupied with his devastating loss, was nevertheless impressed with the speed of the constabulary's response to his report of the crime.

What he wasn't aware of was that Conan had really been sent to investigate the root cause of a recently reported explosion. Doyle licked the tip of his standard issue pencil and poised it over the page of his regulation pocket notepad.

"I think it's those brats, the kids, they're behind it. They've pulled down my alarm cable, forced the lock on my aviary and made off with three of my prize birds."

Doyle attempted a vague interest, but really was perplexed, unsure of exactly what to write and even more unsure of what to say.

"Are you sure?"

"Of course I'm ruddy sure. The cage doors were left wide open and the birds gone. Who else would have done it?"

Perhaps now, in hindsight, Doyle's suggestion was unwise. "A fellow pet collector?"

"Pet! Pet! Do you mean specialist breeder?"

Doyle swiftly back-tracked and nodded as Percy ranted on, "No, they would have been more sophisticated and anyway, they'd never be able to show them. No, it's the village kids I'll wager; so what are you going to do about it?"

It seemed to Doyle that he had made a huge professional error in not investigating the explosion instead. The saviour of the moment was Doris, grasping a tray laden with precariously balanced crockery,

"Tea, Conan?"

"That would be grand," he volunteered in desperation to change the subject. "There's nothing better than a nice cup of tea and a digestive to help put the world to rights."

Doris assumed that the two men had reached an end to their questioning. As far as P.C. Doyle was concerned, her timing was immaculate, but Percy just stood up and, ignoring the freshly-brewed tea, said to Conan as he left the room, "You find these criminals Doyle and I'm off to find my birds."

He slapped three photographs of the cherished beauties on the footstool in front of Doyle and left the room. Doris, obviously deeply worried, told Conan that since the birds' disappearance, Percy spent every spare moment up in the churchyard calling out for his birds to return. He would take an empty cage, a millet spray and one of the more colourful, vocal female budgerigars in her cage and systematically scour the surrounding trees and hedgerows with his binoculars.

"He seems to think they'll come back," Doris explained "He's determined not to let up until he has found them. I've never seen him like this before, he's a broken man. Over the years I've not always been there for my Percy," she confessed.

Conan thought he sensed a touch of remorse in her voice.

Chapter 12

Seth had been protective of Dilly over the years since her mother had passed away, watchful and wary of whom she saw and with whom she spent time. He had told her repeatedly that she was the best thing that could have happened in his lonely life and clearly he held dear her care and devotion to him.

Her heart had never been lost to anyone. All her life had been spent in this place; here was where she grew up and this was all she knew, all she remembered and all she loved. When she lay on the warm sand of the dunes watching the clouds overhead, feelings of happiness and tranquillity washed over her. The summer heat of the pebbles and the chilling freshness of the sea exhilarated her. She loved the silence of the summer when all might happen, but nothing ever did. Sheer pleasure thrilled her as she watched the flocks of thousands of migrant birds lift high from the marshlands at the start of their long journeys to distant lands knowing that, one day, they would return. She adored the wonderful sense of peace as she listened to the sound of rain on the roof of their little cottage, accompanied only by the sound of their old kitchen clock, its note deep, safe and homely. To lean out of her bedroom window on a summer's evening and watch the orange moon rise up above the silver, shining sea, as the brilliant beam of the Light repeatedly swept across the shingle foreshore and white dunes, was magical. On crystal-clear nights the heavens would reveal their secret: hundreds and thousands of distant stars, each with a story to tell.

She loved to watch the seasons come and go but most of all she loved the storms, as long as she was tucked up safely in her home. The air would be fresh and cold, the wind would strengthen as a storm gathered far out to sea, its bright forks of lightning would reach down from the leaden sky again and again and the awakened earth would rumble in reply. This was her paradise, all she had ever wanted.

Dilly set out across the beach, her mind confused. When you don't know everything, you're at a loss, yet when you do...? She struggled to understand, wondering what she should do next, if indeed anything.

Bernard, dressed in his olive green cords and Guernsey jumper, sat outside in the garden of his shack. In the distance he saw pretty Dilly coming towards him across the dunes. He felt increasingly uncomfortable as she approached: he always did, embarrassed and self-conscious for his lifestyle and, above all, his loathsome brother. To her it was of no importance: she enjoyed their chats passing a while together in the garden, musing as they so often did on the sea, the weather and the sky. As for Bernard, he loved these special moments. Dilly's youthful charm and beauty thrilled him and so much reminded him of his earlier years and his teenage sweethearts. Today, though, it was different. Her frivolous nature surprised him. She was excited like he'd never seen her before, like a butterfly that was unable to settle. One minute she appeared frustrated, the next overjoyed and marvelling at how wonderful life was. Bernard plucked up courage and asked her what was troubling her.

"I have met someone, someone special," she hesitated before adding just a single word, "but... "

"But what?" delved Bernard, realising her apprehension in saying more.

Axel appeared in the distance, striding out over the dunes towards them. Having seen Dilly, he was intent to speak with her.

"It's the stranger, isn't it?" Bernard felt confident to judge. "From my garden I've seen you both wandering along the shore and spending many an hour together, talking and laughing."

She didn't think anyone had seen them or knew of their precious moments together.

"I am pleased for you, my dear Dilly," said Bernard. Yet before the words had barely sunk in, she, in a trembling voice, shared, "It's not that simple, he's not what he seems."

Bernard was having none of this guarded talk. "Which of us is? Do you love him? I can see that you do. Does he truly love you?"

She smiled a smile that said it all.

"Well, that's all that matters."

His straightforward approach was always refreshing, but in this instance proved disconcerting.

"Trust me I understand what it is to reject another's love and to spend the rest of your life lonely. There isn't anything else more important than true love."

For a brief moment Dilly thought of Bernard and his brother Carl and, for the first time, understood just how difficult life must be for them both,

"It's not your fault, it's nobody's fault," she tried to reassure him. There are some things that people just don't want to hear and Bernard certainly did not want to hear this.

"I am too old for any of this, too old for sympathy, far too old," and with that the old man stood and said, "Go to him," then bent over and gave her a gentle kiss on her forehead.

Axel's call had caught her attention and Bernard realised Dilly was somewhere else.

"Go on. Go with him. I'll always remember our times together and cherish your company."

She stole across the beach to where Axel was waiting. She clasped his hand and led him to the water's edge just as she had many times before. A growing sense of the importance of this moment filled them both. Dilly felt as if she was soaring swiftly upward, as if flying. It lasted but an instant: the sensation thrilled her. As she thought of the words, she heard herself uttering them, "Will you love me forever?"

"I believe in love," Axel assured her. "Love belongs to you Dilly, and I will always love you."

Overjoyed, they held each other tightly, embraced in each other's arms. No words were shared, none were necessary. The long silence was ended with Dilly's question, "Tell me about your home?"

Axel gathered his thoughts then began to explain.

"Norway, my homeland, is a wonderful place. I lived in a very small fishing haven, north of Stavanger, by forests of spruce, birch and fir, nestled beneath mighty mountains at the head of a deep fjord that cuts into our land, like a valley filled with the ocean. I had an idyllic existence climbing rocky crags and skiing the steep berg ranges with my sisters. My father and I would canoe the fast rivers and we'd fish for trout and salmon in the beautiful lakes, fjords and wild rapids. I'd camp on the remote islands in the bay by breath-taking waterfalls, under night skies. I'd drift off to sleep, enchanted by the sparkling stars overhead. This was my world, shared only with the deer, beaver, bear and lynx. This was my fjord homeland.

"My childhood was a happy one. During the early seasons we'd fish the fjords, split the codfish then salt and hang them on drying racks for our winter store along with our dried mutton. Whaling boats would go out to sea, and I would sit at the end of the jetty, waiting and listening, sometimes for hours, for their return when they would drive pods of leaping, spinning whale ashore where the beached animals would be cut up and shared amongst the village folk. At one time the seas were filled with monster whales: they were as big as the mountains and as peaceful as the lakes, just their song echoed upon the sea-breeze. On many midsummer evenings we would light bonfires, hundreds of them along the banks of the lakes: it was a magical sight. In the autumn we would work in the meadows gathering the harvest while above us the wooded mountain slopes were clothed in rich green, bronze and golden hues. This is the land our great countryman, Grieg, loved. Here he created the music that sings of my homeland.

"On the winter evenings when the chill gripped the air we would gather around the stove in our wooden home. As the icy winds whipped the flames of our fire we'd warm ourselves with hot, wild-berry juice. By the light of the cod liver oil lamp our grandfather would tell stories of sea monsters, hideous beasts that frightened our fishermen; of trolls and other creatures that would run howling and screaming in wild dances through the mountains and valleys, some visible, others invisible, but, to us children, all real. We were enthralled as he shared with us the amazing sagas, tales of the early settlers and the history of our people. When the weather was so bad that not one of us wanted to go out, Father would tell us that there was no bad weather, only bad clothes, then he would venture out into the weather to see to the animals.

"All my happy memories froze when, in the April of 1940, war erupted in our land. Resistance to the invaders slowly grew in strength and many of our people fought to hamper the march of the Germans but they were unstoppable. German soldiers came in their hundreds, in their thousands, and as the Resistance killed Nazi collaborators, the Nazis executed resistance fighters as well as those who tried to flee our country and deported many Norwegians to camps in Germany. If I did not co-operate with them I was told that my family would never see their beloved Norway again."

Axel broke down and sobbed, stumbling over his words,

"It's no use; I must go back." He looked into her eyes. "What are you thinking? What have you been thinking?"

Dilly knew not what to say. Axel spoke again, yearning to know what she was thinking.

"Are you afraid of me?"

Dilly's reply surprised her "I am... I'm afraid *for* you."

"Do you have the heart to still love me?"

Dilly's heart was beating fast. She threw her arms about him, pulling him tightly towards her, her spirit at one with his. She knew one thing: as much as she loved this country, she would have to leave it. "I'll go back with you; we'll return to Norway together."

"What of your father?" Axel asked, hopeful she had considered her words. She assured him Seth would be well looked after by the old women of the village and, after all, he above anyone she knew cherished a life of solitude.

Chapter 13

Seafaring is a calling and in Archie's case it came so loud and clear he couldn't ignore it. Most seamen remember at least one really bad storm: the darkness of the hour, the wild, uncontrollable fury when one's life is in the balance. In spite of the weather being calm, with far reaching bands of mellow scarlet and yellow sunlight burnished across the glimmering sky, Archie was about to journey into probably the fiercest storm he'd yet experienced. The waters, still and reflective, were soon to witness the most outrageous, savage and hostile outbursts. Most battles on the beach were between the two opposing forces of the land and the sea; however, today the battle was between two very different forces – Archie and Timothy.

Archie, having journeyed across the moving mire and the drifting dunes, finally arrived at Timothy's stronghold – his van. There was no evidence that Timothy was prepared for the attack that was to follow, although, in his heart of hearts, he suspected that sooner or later the game would be up. Neither had trained for what was about to happen: their fitness, agility and self-discipline were hardly notable or commendable. Archie charged, not bothering to lay siege to Timothy's fortress, which was little more than a plywood box and ill-equipped as a battleground. The caravan door was unable to withstand Archie's relentless battering and, in one feeble attempt to preserve the hinges, Timothy opened it.

No third party witnessed the blood-letting and torturous fighting that followed, but suffice it to say, Archie was the victor. Timothy's life had been spared, even if his honour and pride were anything but. Usually, at the end of such campaigns, the gallant victor would be rewarded with a knighthood or medal: some acknowledgement of his courage and endeavours. Today was no exception. Word spread far and wide. Timothy had retreated to The Ship to drown his sorrows and to let dear, sweet Molly dress his wounds with TCP and two dozen plasters. As Archie limped across the threshold of his cottage, Stella was there to greet him: not the Stella he knew, but one he vaguely remembered.

Few words were shared: in fact, only nine. Archie's offering followed that of Stella's, "I didn't know you had it in you," to which he added, "Humph!"

After that they went up the narrow, winding staircase to their bedroom and, for the first time in a very long while, had the time of their lives!

Victoria moved her fingers sensually over her body, tracing the line of her firm, young breasts. The eager farm-hand tugged at the buttons of her blouse, ripping the flimsy top from her body. His half-naked frame oozed the rich stench of sweat as he thrust her into the sweet-smelling hay. Trembling with excitement, their bodies entwined, rolling, tumbling together. Caressing her, kissing her again and again he frantically tore at her clothes: Victoria screamed in ecstasy.

Molly put down her book. She couldn't read any further until she'd caught her breath. She had experienced earthy passion at the hands of Tobias, but that was the stuff of innocent peasant girls having babies in cow sheds and would end with one or other, or both, being pushed down a well.

She had come to the conclusion that there should be more to a relationship than just raw sex, yet that was all Tobias seemed to offer. Not, of course, that she wanted to give it up completely, quite the contrary, but maybe a mature man was what she needed. It appeared fortuitous to her that this realisation coincided with Timothy's banishment from the Smart household. Molly peered across the dimly lit bar to where Timothy sat, propped in the corner of the settle beside the open log fire. The Ship's interior was shabby, disagreeable in many respects, a lick of paint being long overdue to brighten the dark bar, but she could have sworn she glimpsed him crying. Molly beckoned him over and, after he'd managed to climb up onto a stool, couldn't help but notice tears running down his face.

"'Tis really that bad?" she asked cautiously. "Surely you'll get over it; he'll be in as much pain as you."

Timothy straightened his back and shoulders and, looking at her full in the face, exclaimed in an inquiring tone, "I don't understand, what do you mean?"

"The tears, I hate to see anyone crying so."

He laughed and, with tears still rolling down his cheeks, replied in a manner not wishing to diminish her concern, "'Tis the fire! I moved from the table where the old boys were puffing their pipes just as a back draft blew down the chimney."

They laughed together, Molly grateful that any tension of the moment had been avoided.

"There's something I must tell you," she said warily. "'Tis something that's not seemly for a lady to say." He looked at her confused and intent on what her words would reveal. "'Twas bound to happen sooner or later." He still had no idea what she was on about. "'Tis all over, well I won't be seeing Tobias again, he'll not be having me in the damp grass up at the church anymore. I'd be after a man who respects a woman." He really wasn't sure where this was all going. "Will you take me out?"

It hadn't crossed his mind. After all, he'd had plenty else to occupy it recently.

"You'd needn't say now and I know 'tain't for a lady to ask," but before she'd finished whatever else was to follow, Timothy replied, "I'd like that."

"Ye'd needn't think I'm desperate, 'cus I ain't. I'd only ever see'd you as a kindly man, a man who 'twas a bit littler than others and maybe a bit lonelier, but still a kindly soul."

She slid her hand over the bar top to rest it on his. With the other he raised his glass of port and slurped nervously. All in all, it had been a funny, old day for Timothy, but just before he got too carried away, he asked one simple, yet important, question of Molly.

"Does Tobias know?"

Another fight, this time with a younger, fitter man, hardly appealed to him.

"Aye, he's been off with a floozy from t'other side of the farm all the time he'd been with me, the pig!"

Well, it all seemed settled, the only formalities remaining were the arrangements for their first, official date or, as Molly described it topping up his port, a chance for a little private cuddle to celebrate. Timothy's blood boiled in expectation like it never had before.

Meanwhile, just a few doors away, Percy had returned from another mission to recover his cherished, warm-blooded, feathered vertebrates without success again. Depressingly, the strong arm of the law, in the guise of P.C. Doyle, had had no success in discovering the evil culprit amongst Doon's criminal fraternity. Percy had no appetite for what was about to await him: Doris's ridicule, the endless tittle-tattle, her hen-like clucking between drags on her cigarette. It was more than Percy could cope with on top of losing the birds.

Doris stood there to greet him. Percy had to take a second glance. Where was the accursed woman he had grown to avoid? Before him was a vision he had not seen in many a year. It spoke in a sympathetic way, something he thought was never possible.

"No luck, my luv?"

Doris was attired in a gaily coloured summer dress. She didn't wear dresses, certainly not ones that revealed her slightly chubby arms and rather scrawny neck and cleavage. She didn't ever wear lipstick! Today, though, she had rubbed bramble leaves with beeswax from the store and coated her plump, juicy lips. Her hair, often in curlers, was brushed neat and tidy – almost styled. Doris had also gone to the bother of collecting ladder-rack at low tide and applied it onto the hard skin of her elbows and heels. She had taken the added precaution of adding a little lavender to overcome its rather unpleasant, lingering smell. For Percy, it was hard to imagine what had brought about this transformation.

"What's wrong?" he pleaded, finding this apparition most disconcerting.

She carefully deflected his understandable confusion, "Nothing my sweet. Now you go on and wash and I'll dish up the mackerel I've fried in oatmeal for you, and pour you a well-deserved pint."

Percy hadn't a clue what Doris was up to but what he did know was that mackerel fried in oatmeal was his favourite. Neither of them, however, had any idea what P.C .Doyle was up to.

P.C. Doyle lounged back in a tatty leather chair and, crossing his hands behind his head, sighed. On the desk in front of him was a communiqué which scared him silly. In a rural constabulary such as this, it was rare to receive anything vaguely concerning. Most of his time was spent with gas mask training, undertaking firearms collections, tracking down lost evacuees, hunting the occasional housebreaker and tackling the odd fight between service personnel in the market town. He couldn't remember anything like this turning up before. Yes, there had been a bomb scare, but just the one and that turned out to be a farmer uncovering an old fuel tank in his field. Little happened these days. There were strange goings-on along the coast, true, but he never got involved in that.

The report had originated at Constabulary HQ over the other side of the county. It appeared as if everyone had had sight of it, including the Chief Constable. Chief Super had passed it to the Super who'd sent it on to Conan's governor, and now it had landed on his desk.

"It's on your patch," the Sarge told him.

An inexperienced police war reservist sauntered into the office brandishing a cuppa for Conan.

"Everything all right boss?" he queried, not waiting for an answer. "They say we should expect raids anytime now!"

Conan had picked up the report and was reading it for a second time. As he perused it, he recalled a quotation his father had shared with him when, as a lad, he'd spent many an hour reading and absorbing the exploits of Sherlock Holmes.

"It is my belief Watson," Holmes stated, *"founded upon my experience, that the lowest and vilest alleys in London do not present a more dreadful record of sin than does the smiling and beautiful countryside."*

Conan rocked forward in his chair, leant on his desk and wondered what to do next. He sipped at his mug of lukewarm tea. A lone housefly buzzed around, bothering him, and then settled on a sticky wax fly-strip he'd hung by the window the day before. He returned to the reports.

A group of five birdwatchers, Edwin Bragg, Sidney Doswell, Bunty Skinner, Dot Storey and Rosie Graydon, had observed strange goings-on by the Ley located beyond the marshlands of Doon and near the secret military station. They explained that they would often come to this large, freshwater lake to observe the wild fowl as the Ley was an important stopping post for passing and over-wintering birds. At this time of year things were usually quiet: the young birds were now more independent and it was well before the migrant birds gathered to head south.

The group had, as was their normal practice, dispersed to three locations about the edge of the lake and waited in silence, studying the bird movements on the water. Through their high-powered binoculars they were able to observe the shape, plumage and antics of the various ducks, geese, gulls and grebes. On the far side of the lake they saw a man with a large, camouflaged Bergen on his back, behaving very strangely. He crawled amongst the reeds, along one of the lake's narrow inlets which reached behind the Listening Station, then disappeared out of sight and they swore that shortly afterwards the air rang with a loud boom. The blast was enough to scatter the flocks of birds in every direction and, try as they might, they never again saw him. The sound of the explosion had indeed been noticed by the Station and reported that very same afternoon, but they thought it sounded a little way off. Rosie Graydon, the leader of the bird-watching group, a prim and well-spoken lady in her early sixties, had been most adamant in her neatly-written statement that all of them thought they recognised the man: he wasn't from Doon they were sure, but they'd definitely seen him about before.

What was more worrying was the other report that was attached. Army Field Headquarters, some thirty miles east along the coast, had advised the Constabulary two days earlier that fifteen Mills hand grenades had gone missing from their ammunitions store.

P.C. Conan Doyle was on to it with the might of the entire Constabulary behind him. The budgie case would have to wait until he'd got to the bottom of this latest crime and brought in his man, and quickly, before something rather nasty happened.

Chapter 14

Equally on the case, although he didn't know it, was Seth. He was about his daily light-keeping chores, cleaning the baffles that split the lantern's beam. The lantern, constantly illuminated, floated and revolved on a pool of mercury – half a ton of it. The mechanism for turning the lantern had to be wound every hour and, consequently, Seth had developed the appropriate muscles to raise the weight that drove the mechanics up through the centre of the tower. Every four seconds its beam would reach out to sea – eighteen miles – a marvel of modern day engineering Seth thought and, as he did so, pride would swell up within him.

A daily task was to wash and polish the large windows which ringed the Light. Seth carried bucket after bucket of water up the one-hundred-and-sixty-nine spiralling stairs, past the radio room, lens room, weather room and service room to the great lens room. Then, carefully reversing down the dark, tightly-winding top steps, he'd descend. A foot pump was used to force the oil from the ground tank to the lamp, whilst white paraffin was needed to fuel the hurricane lamps and coal for the Rayburn, six tons of it a year had to be lifted. And then there was water for cooking and drinking, not that Seth drank much of it other than in his tea and cocoa. The majority of his drinking was concentrated on the most noble of drinks, a malted elixir of the finest breeding and quality, carefully matured in oak bourbon barrels and judiciously bottled for his pleasure.

He was a dishevelled, rangy-looking man, well on in years. He'd looked old for a long while now, but there was no doubting his fitness. The rigours of the job and the weather had well and truly left their mark. Not that Seth had to do this all by himself: there would often be a relief keeper to help but, for whatever reason, they never stayed long. Seth saw to that. Throughout, he never left his post: after all, it was his Light! So, understandably, it was he who, when wandering about his watch emptying the thunder bucket from the balcony, discovered the birds. It certainly wasn't unusual for migrating birds, attracted by the light on stormy nights, to dash themselves against the glass, resulting in instant death. In fact, on the occasions when a duck or goose had met its end in this way, Seth would assist its earthly departure via his Rayburn and dinner plate. What was particularly unusual in this instance was that they were budgerigars: three brightly coloured ones, as dead as you like. He'd never seen anything like it before. They must have flown across the Atlantic or something. What Seth failed to notice as he emptied the Elsan and dropped the budgies onto the rocks below was that thin metal bands ringed the leg of each bird.

For many, Seth's life would be seen as a continual round of monotonous drudgery, day after day suffering solitary, confined and Spartan conditions in a wretched place, thrust out on the edge of the sea and experiencing some of the worst weather imaginable. But for Seth it was wonderful. Here he had all he ever wanted, for this was Seth's world from where he could look down on the other world, the real world, but not a world Seth had much to do with.

From the top of his tower he could see all he wanted. The beach below could appear barren, but he knew it was teeming with life amongst the weed and shingle, burrowing and flourishing on the dune slacks or wading the marshes. As the seasons came and went the colours and hues that met his eyes varied and changed. Silver-grey ribbons of sea purslane wound across the marshland and a variety of coloured blossoms amassed on the dune tufts, carpets of sea kale and the sea poppies, bright, butter-yellow splashes of colour gathered about the shingle. The onshore winds brought a fresh vitality reshaping the dunes, shifting the shingle foreshore and creating new patterns in the relentless sea. If the pebbles were too large for the sea to move, they were battered and ground until they became small enough.

He loved the great storms that ravaged the coastline with the pounding gales and the driving, torrential rain, as long as he was safe in the Light. The skies that warned of an impending onslaught still amazed him, and then there was the lightning and thunder which he found exhilarating – wondrous. At times, when the weather was calmer, the beach appeared to take on a new life. All manner of birds foraged and nested along the shore and circled playfully in the cool air. Oystercatchers and plovers followed the receding tide in search of food.

Rabbits ventured out from their burrows in the mature dunes and feasted on the vegetation. They were not the only harvesters Seth had seen. When old Charlie was about he'd regularly comb the foreshore for whatever might be useful, collecting plants he could use or gathering birds' eggs. He'd always look up and greet the Light with a wave and Seth would wave back.

Seth had witnessed the building of the Listening Station ten or more years past. He'd seen the engineers arrive on site and endless materials and supplies brought in by the little train which trundled on its narrow lines between the marsh and the dunes. He'd observed lorry after lorry with shrouded lights coming and going in the dead of night and then the next morning, all looked deserted, dead but yet somehow different. Buildings and structures were born under cover of darkness. One of the Trinity House inspectors had told Seth that he understood the Station was part of the Acoustic National Early Warning System designed to detect engine sounds of invading hostile aircraft, should they ever come, and Doon was chosen because it was one of the quietest spots in Britain.

That was long before the war and the chap had sworn Seth to secrecy, a demand he had no problem keeping. He didn't understand it anyway. To Seth's eyes the mirrors and buildings had long looked silent and abandoned, isolated and mysterious; it had been a while since the scientists and technicians had left. They no longer stood on the platforms in front of the huge concrete ears for hours on end, working some sort of sophisticated apparatus in all weathers. He assumed they were listening to echoes from the sky.

Now it seemed as though the Army engineers were back in force and with ships. The little train was on the move again but this time its engine was heavily armed with twin anti-tank guns. To Seth there seemed to be something far more sinister and serious about this development. Work was afoot, digging a massive trench inland to somewhere, and a monstrous vessel, the likes of which he'd never seen before, was anchored off-shore. For a fleeting moment Seth thought it was the French again. A relief keeper thought he had seen the ship before when stationed at Lundy's South Light, 175 feet above Hell's Gate, off the north coast of Devon. There he had observed what he considered to be a strange freighter running a massive floating cable drum across the Bristol Channel to near Ilfracombe, some twenty-four miles east of them. It turned out that it had been laying a pipe between there and South Wales, through which fuel could be pumped. And he believed that this was the very same craft.

A new sense of secrecy seemed to surround these developments. Suddenly the block buildings in the compound were heavily camouflaged and more buildings were completed over a dozen or so nights. Soon an elderly barge joined the ship and moved close by. To Seth's trained eyes its superstructure was most peculiar. He concluded there was little sense in speculating the crafts' purpose; he'd just have to wait and see what happened, wondering if he already knew more than it was healthy to know.

Beyond the Station, some seven miles distant from the Light, was one of the many Martello towers that skirted this part of the southern coast. A remnant from the beginning of the last century, this ancient, coastal, war-watching defence still served a purpose. Although only forty feet high, with the combination of Seth's powerful lens and his high vantage point, he could just make it out when the weather was clear. When the weather became inclement, the mournful mist closed in, swallowing all, and sight of the tower was lost. That was the signal for Seth to start the foghorn. Its deep resounding blast, every two minutes, seemed to shake the Light and the very rocks upon which it had stood all these years. He loved the feel of the horn shaking the air, its sense of power and purpose. It comforted him to think that no shipping could fail to hear it.

An occurrence which took place much closer to Seth's observatory could hardly go unnoticed. Timothy's caravan, normally still and peaceful, appeared to have taken on a new lease of life. For some people, sleep heralds all sorts of ideas and thoughts which can grow completely out of all proportion when reality gives way to imagination. Timothy was one such person. His nanny had always told him he was a blessed little boy and one thing he was blessed with in abundance was a vivid imagination – an imagination which, when asleep, meant that he had difficulty distinguishing between what was real and what was not. Once he even imagined he'd had a growth spurt. But now that was no longer a problem: he'd never before known such a good night's sleep when he finally got down to it. Molly Lund had moved in! Molly was snuggled into the downy depths beside Timothy in his intimate bunk. Seth had guessed something was up when he'd spied Molly popping round so much, bringing bags and cases. The rascal! And now, out of the blue, a tatty grey Morris Eight had appeared from nowhere. He had no idea what the two of them were up to: he certainly never suspected they were about to hitch the caravan onto the car and make away, nor that soon towns and villages would resound once again to Professor Lorenzo's 'revived' Punch and Judy Show.

Once a year Seth would go to the bother of smartening himself in preparation for his annual visit to The Ship at Doon. The reason for this rash endeavour was the celebration of a birthday. Yet this occasion was not to remember Seth's progressing years, perish the thought, but something far more important than that. It was the birthday of the Light and this year it would be forty. That's worth toasting, he thought as he savoured a tot of mediocre whisky all by himself on a bench outside the pub. The sky had turned from a magnificent gold with the setting of the sun, and now an arc of fire seemed to burn along the rim of the horizon. The Light stood proudly by, surveying all, as it had for so many years.

Seth's thoughts turned to Dilly. The only thing that was important to him was her happiness. Recalling her smiling face, he chuckled to himself.

Chapter 15

P.C. Doyle had wasted no time. He was hot on the heels of the villain and intended to apprehend him before there was another explosion, probably one many times worse than the first. The boys at County were liaising with the army, but according to Super, not having a lot of joy. He said something about internal investigation. Conan felt as though it was all down to him, which was little comfort when you know the only resources at your disposal are a bike, a brain and a little brawn.

He'd started his investigations searching the Ley banks and came up with nothing unusual, except for two dead fish. Fish die every day, he told himself, but rarely so far up the bank. No fisherman or animal would have left them there, that was for sure. Next, his enquiries centred on Doon. Had any of the inhabitants seen anything or anybody strange on that day? He came up with a big, fat 'no'. Not much happens in Doon where there were few comings and goings! The whole affair was looking increasingly sinister and, search as he might, he could find no evidence of an explosion. To be honest, he was beginning to doubt the reliability of the witnesses, but then all five corroborated the story and there was nothing to suggest he should distrust their word. All was looking bleak: no angles seemed to present themselves and no hunches seemed worth exploring. Who was there left to question? Just as he was about to give up, he had a tip-off,

"What about the stranger, the young man who lives in Charlie's old shack, he's been acting peculiarly lately?"

Conan seized the opportunity,

"Have you seen him with anybody else?" Conan reasoned that he would have had to have an accomplice to get hold of the grenades somehow.

"Only Dilly," came the unhelpful reply.

Conan knew Dilly. They had grown up and gone to school together and he had always had a soft spot for her. He was quite convinced she would never get mixed up in something like this. Before the caller hung up, he had added in a rather dismissive tone, "Of course, that was the day the fish-man comes. He's certainly strange."

The phone went dead.

Conan had only met the fish-man the once after his old pick-up had hit Jim's post-bike, twisting its front forks and buckling the wheel. Undoubtedly, he was a strange man and he had been offhand over the whole occurrence. As if someone had turned on a light in P.C. Doyle's head, he remembered something he thought unusual at the time when searching the lakeside: faint tyre tracks. Perhaps it was a pick-up that had made them: no other vehicles ever went that close to the water's edge. His investigative juices were working overtime. Further enquiries determined the day and time when the likely suspect was next visiting Doon and, if Conan's hunch was right, he would be there to apprehend him before he was able to hurt anyone or attack the Station.

The day came and Conan was ready for anything, or so he thought. His bicycle wheels and chain were freshly oiled to ensure his approach was as silent as possible, the Sturmey Archer gears were running smoothly and the brake blocks checked. He had decided to wear a trench coat over his uniform and a tatty hat so he wouldn't be instantly recognised. In his coat, stuffed down its poacher's pocket, was his truncheon. He had no idea if a fight might be on the cards and was taking no chances! Having had that thought it dawned on him that if this scoundrel used hand grenades, he might well also be armed. That was not a comforting prospect. However, there was little Conan could do about that. He had joined the force knowing there would be dangers that he would have to face: life wasn't all plain sailing. Anyway, he had had his porridge for breakfast. He smiled, appreciating the insignificance of such a thought when faced with a hardened criminal.

Conan had been led to believe that one thing the fish-man could be relied upon was his punctuality. Good news, Conan thought as he pedalled his way to the anticipated crime scene. It was twenty minutes after five. He needed to waste no time as the afternoon was well on and if the fish-man was going to call by on his return from Doon, he felt sure it would be soon. Conan settled himself directly opposite the very location where the bird-watchers observed the man. Sarge, being a bit of an angler and ever so cautious, thought that it was a good idea that Doyle borrowed his fishing rod and some gear so he didn't look conspicuous if spotted. In the increasing cold and dampness of the early evening, Doyle sat silently, waiting.

In an exceedingly grand looking building in the centre of Oslo sat an inexperienced young officer of the notorious German Waffen SS. His office was situated on the second floor of the magnificent Victoria Terrasse which was SS and Gestapo Headquarters. The department in which he served had the most uninformative designation of B7: within the SS it was referred to as Der Handlers. Each day papers and reports on overseas agents would arrive on his and his colleagues' desks. He knew little of the ways in which one handled and worked the Reich's agents. He still had to learn the best methods to keep them committed and engaged in their clandestine work for the glory of the Fatherland. The day had, up to now, proved unremarkable. Junior officers of the SS seldom had anything significant cross their desk. A stack of reports faced him and, as far as he was concerned, they were arranged in no particular order, each as trivial as the next.

Herman Kluge stretched back in his chair, clasped both his hands behind his head and, looking up, admired the ornate friezes that adorned the room's ceiling. Apart from the grand, gilded, stucco wall-panels, the vast office was sparsely furnished with nothing more than one pedestal desk, three chairs and an 18th century chimneypiece. The files were delivered to his office at the start of each day and collected, along with notes and recommendations, at the end of it. There was nothing too demanding, certainly not anything to disrupt his evening dining on fine cuisine and delighting in classical performances at the Conservatoire, now requisitioned by the Nazis.

So it was on this day that one report caused him to sit up and pay particular attention, spending much more than the usual twenty minutes on its consideration. The file was titled 'B7/British Theatre, Southern England Aircraft Detection Developments: Reference 354' and the name that ended the description was 'Axel'. On close scrutiny there was really nothing very earth shattering in the agent's reports, little they didn't already suspect. What was particularly noteworthy was the manner in which his reports, over time, became less informative and valuable, which was quite the contrary to most agents' transmissions: that is, unless they were 'turning'. What was more remarkable was his latest communication and demand. It was a demand he was hardly in any position to make and, in Herman's judgment, was a very unwise action if he valued his and his family's safety. Herr Kluge was convinced this file had found its way into his daily workload by mistake. He had never had 'a turner' before and was not at all *au fait* with the relevant handling procedures.

Axel had been dispatched to the south coast of England, directly across the English Channel from France and the likely location of the German invasion. Intelligence had reached the Third Reich of unusually significant military activity in the region and the installation of substantial antennae and wireless stations strategically guarding the south east coast. One agent referred to them as the Chain, a likely early-warning system. Doon's Station was suspected as being part of this so more information was needed to determine its importance and threat to the German invasion and landings on English soil. Axel's task was to establish the Station's role and initially his reports, detailed and exhaustive, were viewed by the senior intelligence officer as making a contribution to the knowledge the Germans held. But any value had been short lived and now Axel wanted out: he probably thought he had something to trade.

The junior administrative officer knocked twice on Herman Kluge's door before entering on Kluge's acknowledgement. The working day was over and, as was customary, she called to collect and return all files to the basement for safe-keeping. Herman had already decided he would retain Axel's file and slid it into his document case before the administrator had a chance to observe. Having locked his office, he followed her down the three flights of marble stairs, passed through the corridors of interrogation rooms then, bidding her good day, cleared security and stepped out into the chill, evening air. Lighting a cigarette, Herman inhaled deeply. With his heavy, grey overcoat tightly buttoned and its collar turned up, no-one knew who or what he was. He appeared as just another resident of Oslo as he purposefully strode down Ruseløkkveien.

In his apartment, in the absence of any clear orders, he puzzled over what to do about Axel. This was his one opportunity to impress his superiors by taking decisive and positive action, he thought, as he gulped an indifferent glass of red wine. He saw no sense in appealing to Axel or making further threats regarding his parents and sisters – that had already failed. Something had to happen, but exactly what was not clear. Axel was hardly of great importance but he had had contact with other German agents and was familiar with SS communication protocol. His knowledge of the extent and whereabouts of the German occupation forces in southern Norway would also be valuable to British Intelligence. Crucially though, Axel appreciated the significance of this stretch of English coast to the Germans and their future invasion plans. The last thing they needed was him crossing into the lion's den.

The next day, seated at his desk, Herman made a decision that would determine the course of his future career and life. Lifting the black Bakelite telephone handset he dialled the appropriate extension and, after formalities, gave his instructions to extract agent 354. When asked by the officious Kriegsmarine liaison officer holding the phone in the naval office on the floor above, on whose authority this action was approved, Herman unwisely lied. He thanked the naval officer for his co-operation in expediting the problem but by then Herman was talking to a disconnected phone line.

P.C. Doyle pulled his trench coat more tightly about him. This staking-out game was proving boring and he couldn't help but wonder if he was not really wasting his time. The breeze was beginning to stiffen; the cold felt colder. The trees creaked in the wind, their leaves rustling above his head. He could smell the damp, evening air and rotting vegetation. Suddenly, the throaty noise of an engine echoed across the water, shattering the peace. It varied in pitch as the vehicle was clearly making hard-going of the terrain.

A few moments after it stopped, a pair of brilliant headlights dazzled onto the water. Conan started out for the visitor. Although losing his footing and stumbling, he desperately tried to be as quiet as possible. He needed the element of surprise on his side. He tripped over something large, substantial and still and, for a moment in the half light, he feared it was a body. A devilish chill ran down his spine. As he tentatively felt about he soon discovered, to his relief, the' corpse' was a tree trunk.

Without any warning, an almighty explosion shook the air and a second followed almost immediately. Conan was now on the run: the chase was on towards the headlights. He raised his truncheon, swirling it from side to side before him, trying to clear any branches and brambles which he could hardly avoid in this dusk. The sight of a crouched man, frozen in amazement at this unexpected apparition, staring at Doyle as he broke cover, brought Conan to a stop. His charge had been halted by a feeble-looking old chap in a clearing, bent over the bank attempting to net dead fish from the water. The indistinct figure looked up. Chiselled face, hair claggy and wet, the man managed an uneasy smile. As Conan seized the man and hauled him onto his feet in front of the headlights' beam he recognised the fish-man.

Conan opened his trench coat to reach for his notepad and the sight of the uniform made the man even more uneasy.

"I am Police Constable Conan Arthur Doyle."

By now the man was positively shaking,

"Please, I am innocent," he pleaded, "I meant no harm."

Conan made a judgment, not too tricky a one, that all was not well and therefore decided without further ado to caution and cuff the fish-man who was clearly the perpetrator of something illegal.

Following a rigorous line of questioning by Constable Doyle and an exhaustive search of both the man and his pick-up, the not too hideous crime was revealed. In a khaki canvas holdall, in amongst an assortment of crates in the rear of the pick-up, were a dozen hand grenades: grooved, cast-iron cased grenades, looking like pineapples with a ring pull. Conan believed these were the stolen 36M Mills bombs. The fish-man seemingly had taken it into his head that he would supplement his private earnings with some of his own fishing. Not content to enjoy the more leisurely rod-and-line approach, this scoundrel had decided to pursue the more dramatic form: blast fishing.

The blast and shockwaves from a single hand grenade would kill many a fish instantly, causing most to float on the water where they could be easily netted. Conan had never seen the technique used before but could appreciate how simple and ruthlessly efficient it would prove. The stunned fish that floated to the surface he sold at market; the catch that had suffered damage he sold for fish meal. Almost as a gesture, to illustrate his courage, the fish-man explained that he could throw the grenade nearly thirty-five feet but, with only a four second fuse, you had to be sharp on your toes to avoid being hit by the case fragments when it exploded. Doyle winced awkwardly, then glared at him and announced, "I'm taking you in."

On arriving at the police station, villain in tow, Doyle was greeted with tumultuous applause from the officers behind the front desk. A puffy-eyed duty officer took down the particulars but his smiled disappeared and he raised his eyebrows when Doyle confirmed the offence. He rolled his eyes when he heard the word 'grenades'. Conan, on leaving them to book their new guest in for the night, sauntered along the corridor, past the interrogation room, to the staff canteen. He was famished and knew a nice hot cuppa was long overdue. He felt pleased with himself. Another criminal was behind bars. The other lads, already devouring their fill, on seeing him enter tapped their steel cutlery on the side of their plates and cheered loudly. It all seemed a bit too much for Conan and he wondered if Holmes ever got such rapturous acknowledgement of his detective skills. As Doyle queued at the serving hatch, Sarge approached and, slapping him on his back, exclaimed, "Well done lad, you've cracked the crime of the century. Keep that up and you'll be Chief Constable before you know it."

The Sarge's sarcasm had hardly had a chance to sink in before one of the canteen ladies interrupted with, "What will it be Conan?"

He'd had little chance to study the limited menu, but there again it hardly ever changed. Conan was mulling over the merits of choosing spicy bangers and mash or a tasty piece of liver when Sarge saved him the trouble.

"No contest Flo, he'll have fish!" he chuckled. Not content to leave it there, the irritating sergeant added under his breath, "The righteous eats a hearty meal, although it's hardly the crime of the century." But Doyle, by now, was out of earshot.

Chapter 16

Dawn broke grudgingly; a black cloud hung heavy over everything. Spring had long since passed, summer had smouldered and lingered awhile over this place that is Doon and now it was time for autumn to roll in, heralding the early storms of winter.

The barometer's glass had fallen and the wind was backing. The sky looked strange and the clouds had begun to look angry. A storm could be on its way. But, for some unknown reason, against his better judgment and experience, Archie had already set to sea this morning, three and a half hours before the midday high water. Something niggled at him, urging him to go out; he didn't know what it was but go he must.

Boats can die a natural death through old age, decaying on the shore, or they can come to a violent end and that's what Archie, above all else, feared. As the wind freshened, he thought to himself that you couldn't avoid all the storms. Some splinter the boats and wreak havoc with the fishing. Yet he had no idea what this day was to have in store for them.

Billy was up with the lark, keen to take home his fifth share from a good day's catch. To him the weather looked just a bit foxy, not to be trusted. With the uncertain conditions he doubted Archie would set out today, so had devoured a hearty breakfast, one he hoped now to keep down. The sea didn't hold the same magic for him as it did for Archie. The sound of the lapping waves against the side of the hull, the throaty drone of the Kelvin diesel as its dense, exhaust fumes swirled about the deck added little to his enjoyment. There were the weird noises: the clanging of buoys and rigging and the creaking of the timbers and boards as the seas groaned – the mystical music of the sea. This day, however, there would be a different sound, an unfamiliar sound, but one Billy had dreaded. The scourge of soft-skinned, lily-livered landlubbers like Billy: the French called it *mal de mer*. It was the moment when you felt as if your whole insides were trying to escape out of your mouth – 'Aurrah, aurraaahurr.'

They struck out into the surf of the Boil. The surface of the sea was alive. Storm petrels swooped from above, dabbing the water with beaks as they passed over, searching for the oil given off by the shoals. They skimmed the trough of the waves avoiding the growing crests as their long, sooty wings seemed to almost tip the water. Fish twisted and turned, to and fro, some leaping from the cauldron. It was as if the winds had gathered all the fish in the bay to this one spot. The sight of this spectacle thrilled Archie and Billy and, at that moment, they knew it was going to be good, the best it could be. In a frenzy they ran their lines over the side and then it was only a matter of edging *Lively Lady* back and forth. For over an hour they toiled frantically. Every muscle in their bodies ached. Archie had always thought Billy was a good worker: not the brightest of the bunch, but a worker nevertheless.

"I'm sick to the back teeth with these damn fish, when will they stop?" Billy cursed as he started to retrieve the third line.

"Shut it," Archie ordered in a hoarse voice as he slid another full crate across the deck. "Just keep 'em coming lad."

They could smell the fish as the waves lifted and pitched, the boat stirring the waters of the Boil. The sound of the surging waters got louder. The sea became increasingly indistinguishable from the darkening sky. And still the fish kept coming.

Earlier that very same morning, well before dawn, in the occupied northern French port of Cherbourg, a type VIIC Kriegsmarine U-boat waited to put to sea. The crew of fifty-two officers, ratings and commandos lined the submarine deck, some on their first mission, the majority inexperienced and in their twenties. The executive officer spoke first as twenty-six-year-old, bearded Otto von Weismann approached,

"All hands present and accounted for Captain. Watchers at manoeuvre status. The boat is cleared for sea, Sir."

The acknowledgement came, "Thank you number one," then von Weismann turned to the crew, "Well, all set men?"

"Aye sir," each and every man announced in one accord, keen to get underway.

Weismann ordered, "Let's make way."

So it was that 757 tons of German fighting machine silently slipped from its Unterseeboot pen into the hostile waters of the English Channel and onwards to the southern coast of fortress Britain.

Dilly sat curled in her petticoat, snug before the smouldering stove in Charlie's old shack. Axel

massaged her feet before the radiant glow as she sipped her steaming mug of coffee. Her dress was draped across a chair, drying. An hour before, she and Axel were splashing in the foaming surf but then the weather had taken a turn for the worse and they'd chased back to the shack ahead of the rain. Dilly seldom swam as a frightening experience in the bay as a child had put paid to that. She could gather sufficient confidence to tread water and manage a pathetic doggy paddle, but no more. Like young lovers swept up in a whirlwind romance she and Axel played at the water's edge, scooping the sea up with their hands and tossing it over each other. They fooled about, fighting and tumbling in the breaking surf. She was always anxious when in the sea and had great respect for its strength.

Dilly's blonde hair shone with the reflection of the flames that played about the burning driftwood. She should have taken her leave but her emotions convinced her otherwise. Dilly marvelled at Axel and how she had been so soon seduced and fallen in love with him. Tears flowed down her cheeks; it seemed inconceivable that she had so quickly fallen for this stranger. They embraced and gazed into each other's eyes. Axel sighed and, nodding, shared in an anxious voice, "I love you, you know."

"Yes, I know," Dilly said softly. Any sadness she had once known was gone, gone forever. She had discovered a love so strong that it would keep them bound as one together ever more. That's how it will be, she thought. For Dilly everything was just perfect.

Above the white-washed, stone cottages and school house, the general store of convenience, the dingy Ship of drunkards, the haphazard string of dejected clapboard shacks trailing around the shore line and spying into the dim distance was Seth's sole sanctuary – the Light, upright and proudly guarding Doon. Meanwhile, Percy was standing where he often did, in the holy yard of the Lord at Saint Mary and Saint Michael's Church, searching for his cherished birds. His field glasses were pressed hard against his eye-sockets causing him to squint. His area of search had now been extended beyond the hedgerows and trees to the fields, the marsh margins and dunes. Even in this dim light he could still make out the distant, tiny clinker craft of Archie's, pitching out at sea. The boat didn't look its usual red, more a dull ochre, but its stark, white cabin stood out against the grey, leaden sky. The light could play funny tricks on you, he thought to himself.

For a while he gazed towards the black horizon through the grey veil, far into the unknown and wondered what life in France would be like now it was gripped by war.

Captain Weismann gave the order, "Up to periscope depth."

The reply came, "Periscope depth Sir."

A series of orders and responses flowed in quick succession.

"Raise periscope."

"Periscope raised Sir."

"Officer of the watch take the controls."

"I have the controls Sir."

"Helmsman, revolutions six zero, ten down, keep eighty feet, steer zero, three, zero."

The acknowledgement came, "Six knots, ten down eighty, on course zero, three, zero Sir."

"Good," Captain Weismann replied. He had observed no shipping and was now happy to lay a course for their destination.

"Watch, report regular radio and soundings; bosun, commandos to make ready; navigator, maintain heading for Doon, estimated arrival?"

"Twenty-four minutes Sir."

For the men of the Kriegsmarine, this special mission was straightforward: their torpedoes would stay in their tubes. They were used to being at sea in the icy waters of the north Atlantic for months on end: raiders, preying on Allied merchant ships, paralysing the supply convoys to Britain. There they would hunt in wolf packs, submerged by day then surfacing at night to lay siege and destroy the merchantmen and their escorts. Times had been fruitful for them, but German losses were now growing. For these men, on this mission, morale was high.

Percy tucked into his picnic tea. It was fair blowy and had turned cold with a nip in the air. These days Doris would send him off with a piping-hot flask of coffee and sandwiches made from the best bread and tinned spam in the store. He wasn't at all sure what had brought about this change of heart, nor why she had started calling him 'darling'.

Again von Weisman ordered periscope depth. An approach under cover of darkness would have been best but wisdom got the upper hand when approaching this shifting foreshore: some daylight for the raid was essential. As fortune would have it, this storm-laden day offered more cover than Otto had expected and certainly more than the commandos could have hoped for. They had reached the English coast without detection. Having scanned the empty horizon he set the periscope to high magnification and focused on the desolate and deserted shore. The swell was whipping the sea into a frenzy. In an authoritative tone, von Weismann gave his orders.

"Stop all ahead, Officer of the Watch surface the submarine."

"Surface the submarine Sir," the ordered man confirmed, and slowly the 220 foot monster came to the surface.

Percy had settled himself in the shelter of a tree, beneath Mary's nightmarish bough. From here he could command a good view of the far-flung countryside, the beach and sea beyond. He'd still not given up hope of finding his champions. He tucked ravenously into Doris's picnic and on biting one of Archie's pickled onions, vinegar squirted in his eye – irritating and stinging. With that the onion heart shot out of the outer skin that Percy's teeth were anchored into and disappeared into a thicket, an unpleasant event which Percy had unwillingly participated in, albeit one that made him laugh, a rare occurrence for our Percy. He was rubbing his eye intently when he could have sworn he saw something in the bay just off the beach. For an instant something had glistened in the failing light. As he adjusted the field glasses, then removed them to wipe his eye again with a handkerchief, he began to scour the sea. Of course he could easily have been mistaken. Over the past days several times he had been convinced that he'd spotted his birds. No, he decided, as he wheeled the focus screw back and forth, something was there and it was moving. It was so very hard to tell. A swell such as this was well able to hide many a craft as it fell into the sea's sinking troughs.

It was devilishly hard to make out but Percy considered it to be a rubber dinghy with maybe three or four men on board, probably in black wetsuits, he wasn't sure. The inflatable was making for the shore but where had it come from? He stood, steadying his old, service glasses against the tree trunk and concentrated hard. Finally, after several minutes, he pin-pointed a dark shape like a small tower further out: it couldn't possibly be, could it? He didn't want to entertain the idea. But then the waters fell away about it and a thin, black deck-line, several hundred feet long he reckoned, of a submarine sitting just below the surface was revealed.

"Any joy, my brother?" Dunbar enquired, not realising just how much he had surprised Percy with his unannounced presence. And, if that was not enough, Prince was at his heels, and then on Percy's leg, having taken a fancy to some scent or other.

"He'll not bite; he's fussy about who he bites. He doesn't just bite anyone you know!"

Prince whimpered and made an attempt to snap at Percy's heel but it was half-hearted and Percy encouraged him to change his mind with his boot.

"I've seen a rubber dinghy out there," Percy pointed towards the sea.

Dunbar interrupted and spoke, "More fool them. It's a dirty day and not one for a dinghy cruise." He humphed under his breath.

"You don't understand. It's a dinghy heading for the shore from a submarine!"

Dunbar was hardly swift with his dismissal, but eventually a dismissal came.

"No, surely not, I think you've been looking far too long through those binoculars of yours Percy."

"I know a submarine when I see one. I was in the navy, I've seen hundreds. Take a look if you don't believe me," Percy challenged, certain that Dunbar couldn't resist the invite, being a fellow navy man.

"My God, you're right, a damn submarine" and, focusing the glasses to suit his bespectacled eyes, he screamed, "It's a German one!" Dunbar was rarely given to screaming anything so it certainly made an impression on Percy.

Several minutes were given over to what exactly they would do next, after which each set about their tasks. The plan was that Dunbar would handle the phone calls whilst Percy, in true military fashion, would continue to undertake surveillance. The first call was to P.C. Doyle. It was no good ringing the station. Thomas knew you had to call him at his rented cottage, but what he didn't realise was that Conan was fast asleep in bed after a late shift. The phone beside his bed rang for the sixth time: obviously this caller was not about to give up.

Conan was ill-prepared for such an interruption to his slumbers. He struggled with his eiderdown and pillows and knocked over the clock as he reached out for the handset. At the first mention of a submarine his brain was hardly functioning, but with the repeated report, and Dunbar's insistence, Conan began to take note. The reverend was not renowned for fantasising or having hallucinations. The words, "You must come, and come immediately," caused Conan to shake his head in disbelief and say, "I am on my way."

Yawning widely he began to wonder if a tragedy was in the offing: he concluded the tragedy was that he was no longer lying in bed. Dressed – he had no time to wash – he wheeled his regulation bicycle from the shed, switched on its lights, adjusted his helmet and a perplexed P.C. Doyle set off on his thirty-five-minute cycle to Doon. Thomas, pleased with his success to date, telephoned Miss McWalters at the school and told her to bring the children up to the church for safety. Lastly, he called 'DOON 1', The Ship, and asked them to spread the word throughout the village, adding, "You can get a really good view from the churchyard."

Percy was still scrutinising the seascape, aware that these U-boats often hunted in packs.

The little village was a hive of activity. A right old melée broke out in The Ship after the call before men hurried out muttering "Submarine" in a disbelieving way. Someone at The Ship phoned Doris and, with the news, a commotion like she'd never known before ensued, then ended as quickly as it had started as her customers left the general store, scurrying home grumbling about the Germans.

The old fisherman had stopped knitting a funnel for a lobster pot and, getting to his feet, murmured, "What's that you say? A rubber dinghy?"

The old women of the village were occupied repairing and baiting the long lines for another day and were heard to complain, "Soldiers? Here, on our beach?" as they gathered up their things.

Stella Smart, busy re-pegging her smalls on the garden line, taking full advantage of the blow, caught the word and, in utter disbelief, cried aloud, "Save my sailor. Come back Archie." She ripped off her pinny and, striding down her path, joined the others heading up dusty Maid's End Lane to the church.

Parading at the head of the village exodus was proud Miss Philippa McWalters and her class, a testament to her dedication and discipline: orderly, calm and of exemplary behaviour, each thinking to themselves, "What's a submarine?"

High above, from his window on the world, behind his spy-glass on the sea, sad, old Seth had seen everything. He remembered his wife, how beautiful she was, and how lovely their daughter had become, and it was the beauty and independence of Dilly that reminded him of her mother. He had seen her with the stranger. It gladdened his heart, but he was sad for himself for he knew he had lost her forever.

Seth had seen the submarine break the surface of the sea, seen the commandos take to the water and now they were landing on the beach, by Charlie's shack, and running to where Dilly and the stranger were. He was agitated, beside himself. It was insane but what could he do, after all he was only the lighthouse man. With that revelation, he heaved back the cover that shrouded the powerful lens from the sun's rays and lit the big light.

From the high hill, not far away, the villagers saw the light. Dunbar had climbed the tower of his church and begun to peal the ancient bells. Seth heard nothing of this for he had, by now, started the foghorn and its haunting, warning drone echoed around the bay.

Chapter 17

The shack door burst open suddenly and two men charged in, pistols drawn. A third smashed open the rear door, splitting the frame where the lock case was secured. Axel panicked. Dilly was beside herself as they seized him, brutally knocking him to the floor and shouting at him in German as their punches exploded into Axel's gut. Try as she might she could get no sense from them. Axel was now clearly pleading for his life. The two men had succeeded in restraining him, binding Axel's hands, whilst the third appeared to be looking for something. Dilly hurled herself at him trying to bring the man down, but he pushed her to one side effortlessly, violently landing her a kick as she fell. She begged the soldier who stood over her to let Axel go, but he was having none of it. He hit again, this time with his pistol butt to her head. Dilly's body slumped, semiconscious. When, a few minutes later she came fully to, the hut was empty. The men had gone and so had Axel.

After Axel had told the Germans that he would no longer help them, he thought there would be repercussions of sorts, but neither he nor Dilly expected this. She stumbled out of the shack onto the shore and froze in horror to see four figures in a dinghy, heading out to sea – one had to be Axel. She knew it was and she knew she could not bear to lose him.

Dilly ran barefoot across the shingle towards the crashing waves, her heart pounding and she wept as she ran, turning over and over in her head, "Nothing will take him from me, I'll never let him go." She stopped at the water's edge and stood hoping, waiting for the nightmare to end, but it didn't.

Archie hadn't seen the submarine: he and Billy were too busy coping with their catch and the challenging sea, or at least Billy had been until Archie saw him retching over the side, watching the departure of his greasy breakfast on the next wave. Archie could feel the boat shake with the sea's power, the thundering swell and the squalling wind. Had he left it too late? He cried out to Billy who seemed frozen, bent over the side as if in a spell.

"You've got no time for that, Billy Richards." Archie hoped that by using his full name, something he rarely did, he might get Billy's attention. "No point in you staring over the side, there's work to be done!"

He hoped that the less-than-sympathetic approach would do the trick. Just as Billy was about to pull himself away he screamed out in disbelief, "There's a hog, a bleeding great whale," and pointed for'ard.

Archie really didn't have time for the lad's ailments one minute and vivid imagination the next. The driving, salty wind made it hard to see anything clearly, but there certainly seemed to be something there. As they motored on, *Lively Lady* disappeared below rolling waves, the sea drenching her deck, then rose up and shook herself before the thick beam of the fishing boat forged on, ploughing through the swell like a beast of the sea.

Billy shouted again, "There's the monster," and then, as if by some evil twist of fate, they both realised it was a submarine, a German U-boat, its ensign clearly visible.

A tireless wave rose and crashed against the U-boat, earthy-yellow foam gathered swirling about its deck as the waters receded. Aloft in the boat's conning tower, a crew hand on watch duty scanning the skyline, thanked God there were no signs of the enemy. Then something caught his eye: a dark shape was visible for a moment then suddenly vanished below the waves. Adjusting his binoculars it only took him a minute before he shouted, "I have a sighting Sir."

"Where?" was the reply, as the Watch Officer turned to train his glasses in the same direction.

"We have a surface vessel Sir, bearing down on us," he screamed to the bridge and Captain von Weismann, giving its bearing.

"A vessel?" Otto questioned.

"A fishing boat. It's coming in slowly but if it maintains its course it will soon be upon us Sir."

"The gun?" Otto asked.

The officer immediately returned, "There's no time for the deck gun Sir!"

The Kriegsmarine submariners were about to get the shock of their lives.

"Clear tower, prepare to dive."

"Aye, aye Sir," came the reply of the watch crew as they unhitched their safety lines. The last below clamped down the watertight hatch as the sea poured in, soaking him as he descended to the bridge.

"All hands. Dive. Dive," the command rang out and the klaxon blasted once, then again.

"Take her down Number Two, steer course one, eight, zero."

"Shut main decks, all hatches dry, shut main vents," demanded Otto's Number Two.

The for'ard hydroplanes were set down and maximum speed attained.

"Diving on course Sir, coming to one, eight, zero. All main decks and vents indicating shut Sir."

"Go to red lighting, blow all main ballast."

"Blowing Sir." The bow pitched down.

"Flood forward trim tanks."

"Forward trims flooded Sir."

As the U-boat dived steeply its stern rose, the propellers coming out of the water and, for a moment, the submarine stopped as if frozen in time; then it started to slide slowly down.

Bells echoed throughout the craft. Men raced up and down the walkways between the rows of bunks from which others had tumbled out, each making for their station. It was increasingly hard to see anything clearly under the flickering lights. Men playing cards threw their hands in as the record-player's arm skidded across the recording. One unlucky officer was caught with his pants down, seated on the toilet. The men, who had one of the toughest and most dangerous jobs were busy having a salt-water, sponge bath. Their prized bottles of Kolibri cologne slid across the torpedo room and smashed.

"Action Stations," von Weismann demanded.

"Action Stations, Action Stations," bellowed over the tannoy.

"Shut off for attack, ready all tubes." The torpedo men worked frantically.

"Tubes one and two charged Sir."

"Flood tubes one and two."

"Tubes one and two flooded Sir, tubes equalised."

"Bow caps and watch your depth Chief."

"Bow caps open Sir. Depth steady Sir."

"Periscope up."

"Up periscope Sir."

Captain Otto von Weismann's heart sank. Being rammed by a boat, no matter what size, was one of the worst fears for a submarine commander. The fishing boat was almost upon them.

Archie could just see the conning tower above the waves and knew if the old engine would hold out they could have the rogue. The two men now worked together, each knowing what they had to do. Archie manoeuvred the tub and Billy retrieved the last of the lines, shifting a drum of diesel fuel across the deck to the boat's starboard side. Waves crashed against the boat's gunwales, tails of salt spray whipped into his face. Archie had fully opened up the Kelvin: it roared and choked, fumes belching from its exhaust. The old girl was struggling against the swell for all she was worth. Archie knew they had to do something and was determined this one was not going to get away if he had anything to do with it.

"No point in you thinking you can hide down there: that's the place for the dead," Archie muttered under his breath as he grappled with the wheel to keep her bearing down on the sub. It was strange, for it didn't feel as though he was any longer steering the craft. A smell of paraffin filled the wheelhouse as the hurricane lamps swung erratically scribing arcs with the movement of the craft, spilling oil onto the discarded sou'westers and Mae Wests heaped on the cabin floor. They powered on in anticipation that this was it: *Lively Lady* was destined for an honourable death. Nothing to regret, nothing to bring shame: she would get her 'kill' even if she had to follow it to the murky depths. And still the little fishing boat ploughed on.

At the time the boat struck there was the loudest sound Archie and Billy had ever heard. A great column of water threw the matchwood of the starboard gunwales high into the air. The boat lurched heavily to port yet *Lively Lady*'s strong, broad bow still didn't yield. It wasn't the most perfect of attacks Archie thought, but then it was good enough to do some serious damage. Survival now totally occupied his thinking. He drew a deep breath, wiped his forehead with the back of his hand and, whilst appreciating that death is never far away, waiting at one's shoulder, concluded that in all his years as a captain, he'd never lost a boat or crew member before and wasn't about to now.

Crates of fresh fish had been hurled overboard, their oil spreading across the water, proving too much for the shoals of dogfish to resist which were now tearing wildly at their flesh. Overhead the gulls screamed in bizarre protest at the frenzy, the strong smell of fish more than they too could ignore. The drum of diesel fuel, having rolled over the side, was on its way down, seeping its thick oil as it followed the sinking submarine. Archie had brought the *Lady* about and, taking advantage of the currents, was attempting to put as much distance between them and the submarine as possible: something told him that it wasn't all over yet. He thought of Stella, comforted that she knew nothing of what had happened.

The whole, thick, grey sky unexpectedly filled with a vast sinister flame, like a huge burning mass. The sea shook and spoke and, for one brief moment even the waves ceased. A deafening blast rang in the air and an explosion spewed from the depths, belching steam and throwing forth debris. Archie was hit and fell back, cracking his head on the wheelhouse door where he lay, crumpled. Splinters from the boat's super structure flew in all directions and part of its mast was ripped from the deck. As quickly as a fire broke out in the wheelhouse, a great wave washed over the starboard side, almost casting Billy overboard, and flooded the boat, quenching the flames. *Lively Lady's* faithful engine spluttered and choked. Then, as if in protest, it stalled. But still the loyal craft stayed afloat.

Seth, on hearing the explosion, was grateful that he was safe on the rocks and felt certain the war had, unquestionably, come to Doon. He had seen Archie's boat ram the submarine and, for him, the taste of vengeance was good. If it wasn't the dratted French it was the dreadful Germans he thought to himself as he hummed Tchaikovsky's rousing *1812 Overture*, a favourite of his especially when there was a storm brewing. Its formidable crescendos served well to remind him of the sea's power and he smiled one of his few smiles.

On top of the hill in the churchyard, the village children clapped their hands over their ears and moved from one leg to the other in excitement, hoping not to miss anything. Doris's nerves were on edge. She'd lit a cigarette to help calm them, but on noticing Percy under one of the trees, stamped it out. She knew he couldn't bear to see her smoking. But Percy was not aware that she was there: he was too busy cursing,

"The bastards, dirty, Jerry navy, bloody murderers." Then instinctively, turning to the Reverend Dunbar, pleaded for forgiveness, explaining that his tongue had sinned, but Dunbar was nowhere to be seen. Unbeknown to Percy and, for that matter, everyone else, a crack had opened in the ancient trunk of the big tree under which he stood and, without any warning, the massive bough from which Mary Bell had at one time hung, snapped and fell to within a foot of where Percy was standing. The legend of the hanging tree was no more: nor was Percy, well at least for the present – he'd fainted!

Stella, quietly and earnestly, gave up a word of prayer. It seemed to her quite an appropriate place to do so. She asked that her Archie, a God-fearing man, would be protected from the elements and the fearful enemy and that the Lord would bring him back safely to her. Oh, and that Billy would be all right too.

Thomas Dunbar had dutifully taken himself off to the Manse to comfort Precious in this time of trouble. She, however, no longer knew who he was and incessantly asked him what his name was and what he was doing there. For Precious, the penetrating sound of the church bells, the moaning foghorn with its blinding, flashing light and the screaming children in the yard had all been far too much for her to bear. The deafening explosion proved the final straw, convincing her that the end of the world had come. She had completely lost it. Thomas realised this when she told him that she never expected Heaven to be this noisy, then sought confirmation from him that it wasn't Hell she'd come to by mistake.

Police Constable Conan Arthur Doyle paced himself modestly upon his trusty bike as he leisurely made his way down the meandering tracks to Doon. It must be said that the explosion came as quite a shock to him, throwing him off-balance, somersaulting and cartwheeling over the handlebars of his machine and across the ground. Having gathered his senses, he straightened the handlebars, mounted the saddle and pedalled furiously for the village, wondering what he would behold.

Bernard, being half asleep beneath the arbour he had only recently finished constructing in his garden, had been disturbed by the blast. Rising to his feet, it took a few seconds for him to realise something of what had happened. Shuffling, zipping his cardigan as he went, he stopped at the water's edge amazed, gazing in utter disbelief at the scene that lay before him. The sea was alive, bubbling like a cauldron, the air thick and dark with smoke, tentacles of fire reaching high, twisting and turning. An acrid smell hung heavily, the fumes carried on the wind. Bernard's eyes were beginning to water but he was certain he could see Archie's little boat out there fighting against the wild sea and, if he wasn't mistaken, a small dinghy low in the water.

He hadn't yet noticed Dilly staring out to sea, just as he was, further along the shore. Someone else Bernard was yet to see this day was his brother Carl. The genius, the eccentric whose imagination and dreams had become all-consuming, some might even say a madman, had, for an hour or more before the explosion, been engrossed in, of all things, a clock: a clock that had not experienced the passing of time for some while. Seated crossed legged upon the floor of his room Carl, surrounded by stacks of old, unread newspapers, stacks that nearly touched the ceiling, marvelled at the timepiece's mechanism. Feverishly he toiled, accurately re-positioning new springs, meanly oiling dry bearings and checking each wheel and cog. His fingers nimbly manipulated each part: he convinced himself that rebirth would soon come to this old master of time. As Carl turned the substantial brass key cautiously, springs wound, cogs engaged, wheels spun, weights descended, the pendulum swung and the clock's hands moved. Life had returned: tick-tock, tick-tock, and then came an almighty bang that shook the very fabric of their shack. Carl had never known such an explosion before and he would never hear such a one again. The newspaper stack, directly beside where he sat, was the highest and, as it happened, the most weighty of all. At first it only rocked a little, then it started to sway, becoming increasingly unstable. In the end the movement was more than the pile could sustain and hundreds upon hundreds of neatly folded newspapers, their weight more than one could imagine, tumbled on top of Carl, burying him completely. The strange sombreness and misery of his room haunted this dark place. No more would that feverishness pulse through Carl's veins. His fat face grimaced one last time as a dark red liquid started to trickle from the corner of his mouth, running down his chin onto his unruly but grand red bow tie, decorated with white dots which waved from his frayed shirt collar. Carl's obsessive hoarding had finally and, somewhat unusually, been the death of him. As if filled with a second sense, Bernard, standing on the beach, sighed.

Chapter 18

The submarine finally settled on the muddy seabed at a depth of 136 feet. The speed of the submerged U-boat was zero knots.

The men had fearfully battled in darkness, trying to regain control and arrest their rapid descent, as more and more systems on-board failed. The impact, as the boat eventually came to rest, caused a thick layer of murky silt to settle on the craft. The only movement outside of the boat was that of a graceful, waving, mast-head, naval flag, drifting in the sea's currents, and dense streams of air bubbles and steam blowing out of her ruptured hull, rising urgently to the surface. *Lively Lady* had cast her fatal and final blow.

Although they had not come with destruction in mind, everything now seemed to be against them. Hatches were slammed shut as water poured in from pipes and bulkheads and the craft started to list badly. Sea water flooded the battery room and should this mix with the leaking accumulator acid, a gas that the sailors feared most would be produced and would begin its poisonous journey creeping through the boat. Far forward, in the once pressurised hull, was the bow torpedo room. During impact and the explosion, one of the torpedoes had become dislodged from its cradle: now it was jammed against the one bulkhead hatch. The only course of escape remaining for these men was through the top hatch but should they try from this depth then death surely awaited them.

Otto was certain that they had finally discovered their eerie and loathsome grave, the resting place for their iron coffin. He knew that the worst nightmare any man could experience was awaiting them: to be trapped upon the sea floor, to die a horrendous death.

A stoic Captain Otto von Weismann announced to his crew, "If we must die on this day we must die with dignity." But few heard his words as panic gripped the doomed submarine.

Nobody would ever know what he wrote in the boat's log concerning the perils of their mission and the sea.

Chapter 19

How long it was before Dilly waded into the sea was unclear. She was shouting and screaming for several minutes, waving her arms on the shore and jumping, trying hard to get the attention of Axel and the German soldiers in the dinghy, the men who had just seen their only means of escape explode and sink out of sight.

Axel had tried to appeal to Dilly as he was being dragged from the shack telling her that everything would be all right, but she never heard him and anyway, Axel knew better.

As she stood in the water up to her waist, the whole sea stirred and washed over her, drenching her, soaking her hair. Her teeth chattered, more from stress than cold. The strange light silhouetted her against the rising, white shingle foreshore; the stones at its very edge loudly rumbling and grinding with the force of the relentless rollers breaking and playing on her already confused mind. She couldn't bear to lose him. On hearing a distant cry from Axel, carried on the wind, Dilly threw herself into the pounding waves.

"Axel, my Axel," she cried helplessly over and over again. As she floundered in the water, she dreamt of just holding him again and that everything would be all right. They had both loved the sea; now though, the very sea that had meant so much to them was tearing them apart. The merciless waves rolled over her; the vast waters swamped her, thrusting her downwards into the depths, then lifting her up again and again. The freezing cold was biting into her, chilling her very bones. She could feel her strength seeping from her.

Lying soaked in the inflatable Axel worked his wrists, trying to release himself from the rope the commandos had wrapped around them. The cold helped numb any sensation as the restraints tore at his skin, drawing blood. Concentrating on the three men, he plainly saw their dilemma and despair as they appeared to be in disagreement over what they were to do. Freeing himself, he picked his moment, surprising the men by barging them to one side as he dived overboard. The confused Germans were of no mind to pursue as Axel, defiantly, pushed on towards the shore and his love, Dilly.

For Dilly it was a desperate situation. With every stroke she became weaker, her feeble attempts proved hopeless. Axel could see his love struggling to stay afloat but he was still a way off and beginning to suffer from the weight of his saturated clothes and the bitter cold. If only he could reach her before it was too late.

She longed for the cords that had once tied them to draw them together again. She longed for her Axel.

Coughing and choking her last, a pinkish foam oozed from her nostrils and from between the ice-blue lips of her mouth before it was washed away in a moment on the surf. As she started to sink, exhausted, Axel grabbed her in his arms and pulled her to him. He fought, summoning all his energy, attempting to keep them both afloat. She knew she was going home. She felt Heaven was calling her.

Already the flat, leaf-like blades of kelp, their red and yellow ochre fronds reached up to Dilly from the depths. Each wave seemed to increasingly tangle them about her legs, drawing her deeper to their forest home. Just before Dilly's body went limp in his arms, she called his name again and again. Axel spoke to her, "Our love will never die; I will not leave you."

The waters opened and together they were swallowed into the murky depths.

Chapter 20

In his heart of hearts Seth knew he'd lost Dilly sometime before, but not in this way. Living this close to the wind and the waves, the rocks and the sky, he was conscious of just how powerful and dangerous they could be. He had seen everything: seen how final it was and had been unable to help. How wasteful and needless and, for him, it was the end of the best years of his life. He had lost his wife and now he had lost his beloved daughter, the most beautiful thing in his life. He prayed that if there was a better place, she was there, nearer to God where she would find a new peace.

Out of the storm's gloom there moved an arc of fire which burnt low on the rim of the sea's horizon. The sun was setting like a magnificent ring of golden red in the now soundless sky. The wide, luminous, open waters were brilliant and tranquil again. Slowly the night began to hide all from view.

Moment by moment, day by day, month by month time moved on. Even as it moved, it seemed to stand still for Seth as he became no more resigned to his fate.

Seth never lost his memories. They were as vivid now as at the very moment, buried deep in his mind. He took up his pen and, on plain white paper, started another of his letters:

My dearest Dilly,
It's been two long years since those last days in Doon, such a long time ago.

His letter told of the ways of the sea birds, the migrating geese and the wild flowers, the big skies and tiny stars, the restless weather and seas. It told of the end of war and of how soon winter would return. He ended by sharing with her something of the life she loved when on this earth:

I picked this pink flower for you from the top of my rocks which lean out over the sea. It grows in peace in a small crevice away from the rabbit, the gull and the otter. It has a sweet scent. Its roots hold it firm against the winds and waves. It is as delightful and lovely as you are, my dearest child, as precious and delicate, and every time I see it in bloom it brings joy to me.

I greatly miss you my darling Dilly. Stay safe.

Your loving father,
Seth

He rolled the sheet carefully, placing the flower stem in the coiled paper, then slid both into a bottle, just as he had many times before. Warily he picked his steps over the rocks and tossed the sealed, whisky bottle into the foaming brine. Seth sighed heavily.

Hundreds of messages drift out across the seas and oceans, many lost forever.

EPILOGUE

So it is that this swirling tale of life in the tranquil village of Doon, of its curious inhabitants, of loves found and lost, of remorse and of forgiveness, has come to an end. This has been the story of Dilly and her heaven-touched land and the wild untamed sea she knew so well and adored. The story of Doon over that long summer was written about Dilly and of two hearts very much in love. Sometimes these are the hardest stories to tell, but at least, when told, they are never forgotten.

After this, there will be other tales, written on other pages, of new folk who come and old folk who go.

'The sea, the majestic sea,
breaks everything, crushes everything,
cleans everything, takes everything . . . from me

- Corinne Bailey Rae

One Day in June

A young man who had long dreamt of becoming a pilot leaves his home in London and joins the RAF. This story follows his life as a navigator in a Halifax bomber, his brushes with death and his part in dangerous SOE missions. He is shot down over occupied France but finally escapes with the help of a farming family and the Resistance. Years later he returns to the French countryside to find his wartime sweetheart and learns of the terror that had befallen that quiet village.

'Beazley's mastery of historical detail enables him to bring to life this tale of bittersweet love of a young adventurer confronted with the excitement, horror and the uncertainties of the Second World War.'

A Tale of Two Elephants

The tale, as told by a female African elephant, traces her life story from the wildness of the vast savannah and the ruthless poachers that have made destruction of elephants their business, through her time in the circus and finally to a peaceful retreat in a wildlife sanctuary. It is at this sanctuary that a friendship with a male Asian elephant flourishes and the tusker's life story is shared. This illustrated book has an appeal to all ages.

'Through Colin Beazley's sensitive writing, two gentle giants of the animal kingdom are brought to life to share their experiences of living alongside man. Truly an imaginative and evocative tale.'

www.fourboysbooks.com